Jan Turner was born in England and immigrated to Australia in 1990. She is a practicing artist and taught visual arts and photography for over 13 years. Jan is now a clinical psychologist and combines her passions of psychology and the arts. She holds a great desire and interest for the supernatural and is fascinated by the genre of horror.

To my son, Beau, who I love so much and I am very proud of. For my beautiful mum, Joan, and dad, Peter. Thank you for all your love and support always. RIP, Mum, I love you.

Jan Turner

CEDAR LANE

AUSTIN MACAULEY PUBLISHERS™

LONDON • CAMBRIDGE • NEW YORK • SHARJAH

A CIP catalogue record for this title is available from the British Library.

ISBN 9781528933674 (Paperback)
ISBN 9781528933681 (Hardback)
ISBN 9781528967563 (ePub e-book)

www.austinmacauley.com

First Published (2020)
Austin Macauley Publishers Ltd
25 Canada Square
Canary Wharf
London
E14 5LQ

I have been blessed with a wonderful family, and although some of us are separated by over 10,000 miles, they are always in my heart and thoughts. In England, I have my big brother Chris and all his family, and my beautiful big sister, Sue, and all her loved ones. My brother Phil and all his family live here in Australia and we are very close. I am very lucky to have had my parents near and I am grateful for all the love and kindness they have showed me over the years. Unfortunately, we lost Mum in 2017 and we are all trying to deal with that huge loss in our lives. My dad and Aunty Dot are still an inspiration to us all and I love hanging out with my dad. My son, Beau, is truly remarkable and he never ceases to amaze me. He has served for his country and now is pursuing a new career which involves the protection of all civilians. My family makes me feel loved, and I thank them all for their ongoing encouragement in whatever I choose to do.

I want to thank Austin Macauley for giving me this opportunity and for all their help and support in making this book a reality.

To all my friends and colleagues, a big thank you for making my life that much brighter. A special thank you to my friend Jo-Anne, who put up with my weekly rantings about the characters. Her enthusiasm gave me the confidence to complete this story.

1

Brian turned the key, and the engine stirred. He wound the window down, lit a cigarette and drove carefully out of the drab car park. It was 4 pm, and Brian had plenty of time and knew exactly where he was going. This meticulous killer had been surveying his prey for some weeks now. Brian had a good feeling about tonight. *Soon she will be mine,* he thought, smiling as he threw his cigarette butt outside the window. He pushed down harder on the accelerator in anticipation, longing to have this young girl's soft flesh rub up against his own. The traffic was heavy for that time of the evening with streams of cars heading home after a long day's work. Brian arrived in Dukinfield with plenty of time to spare. He pulled into the curb along Dewsnap Lane and switched off the engine. He was far enough away to be out of view, but close enough to keep an eye out for his unsuspecting victim.

The girl was Sandra Ellis, a sweet eighteen-year-old redhead who worked passionately at an elderly nursing facility. She adored the old people and felt really at home there. At 5 pm she would begin her long walk home completely unaware that these precious moments would be her last. Brian waited patiently for the girl to start her ascent along Dewsnap Lane. For Brian, the waiting was part of the excitement, and he could feel a slight hardening in his groin as he checked his watch and it was a few minutes to five. Brian looked at his face in the front mirror and swept his remaining strands of hair over to the side of his balding head. *Come on my pretty girl,* he thought. *I have been waiting for you.*

Suddenly he spotted her walking out of the nursing home. Sandra turned right and was briskly walking up to the lane where she would cross over the main road. Brian drove slowly giving the girl a chance to cross the busy main street ahead. As soon as she was across and walking along the concrete pavement, Brian made his move. He pulled up slightly in front of her and wound down the passenger side window. Sandra looked briefly in his direction. 'Hello there,' he said, smiling as best he could. 'Where are you off to?' Sandra stopped and leant into the car window to get a better look at the driver. She didn't recognise him and thought it was a bit weird for someone to stop like that. Brian could see the look of caution on her face and knew he had to act quickly if he was going to get her into his car. 'Do you need a lift?' he asked.

The young girl took hardly any time to reply and said, 'No, thanks, mister, I've not got much further to go.' Brian knew she was lying as he had followed her home many times in the past and it was a good half hour walk.

'Okay, but I'm heading home to the wife and thought you might fancy a lift.'

Sandra smiled and said, 'No, thanks,' as she continued walking.

Brian sat there for a second as he watched her get further away. His fat sweaty fingers clenched the hard surface of the steering wheel tightly and he bit down hard on his bottom lip. *This is not supposed to happen,* he thought. *She is the fucking one, I know it, and fate led me straight to her. Fucking bitch, I'll show you what happens when you walk away from me.*

Brian stepped out of his car and opened the boot. He grabbed a long-bladed knife and held it underneath his brown suit jacket with his right hand. After locking the car, Brian began walking in the same direction as the girl. Sandra turned her head and saw the strange man walking towards her. She knew something was terribly wrong, so she picked up her pace. Her heart began to beat loud in her chest, and she turned around once more. The man wasn't going away, and he had a vacant look on his face which sent shivers down her spine. She decided to make a run for it. There were no other pedestrians about and even if she made a run to the nearest house, Sandra knew the man would have time to catch up with her. She just kept on running and didn't look back. Brian knew he had to run to keep up with the girl, but he was so unfit. Sandra turned her head once more, and Brian caught the fear in her eyes. Her foot went down into a hole on the pavement, and she lost her balance falling helplessly to the ground. Brian kept on running and soon found himself standing over her. Panting with exhaustion, he knelt down quickly and forced the blade of the knife up against her throat. 'If you don't get up with me now, I'll cut your neck right open,' he said. Sandra looked into his dark, cold eyes and did what he asked. When she was back on her feet, Brian placed his arm around her shoulders and pressed the knife into her chest. 'Just keep walking,' he ordered. Sandra looked around desperately to see if anyone was on the pavement, but there was no one. She stared into the cars that had stopped for the traffic lights trying to get someone to see her. It was useless; she felt totally alone and invisible.

They approached Brian's car, and he unlocked the passenger side first and pushed Sandra inside. While he was walking around to the driver's side, she quickly locked the doors and pushed down on the car horn letting it blast out into the street. Brian tried to open his door, but Sandra was holding down the lock. *The fucking bitch,* he thought. He knew someone would see him if he didn't do something to stop her. He looked around and found a small rock on the side of the road. He grabbed it and smashed it down hard on the driver's side window. The glass shattered into a million pieces, and he reached down to ply away her hands. Sandra was holding on tight and by this time Brian was getting really pissed off. He managed to force her hands off the door lock, opened the door and sat down inside. Sandra wasted no time and opened the passenger side door and started to escape. Brian grabbed her long red hair and pulled down hard, trying to hold the girl inside the car. Sandra struggled but would not give up trying. Brian began to panic about being seen, so he reached for the knife and thrust it into the girl's back. She screamed out in pain but kept on struggling to get free. Brian stabbed her again and again until she stopped.

He made his way around to the passenger side of the car and pushed her lifeless body back into the seat and closed the door. He knew he had to get away from the street and before long he was driving along a secluded road where he stopped to think. *Jesus fucking Christ, what the fuck has just happened? She was supposed to be the one and it was not meant to happen like this.* Brian looked down at the dead corpse now on his passenger seat and the floor, which was covered in blood. His driver's window was smashed to pieces and it would be getting dark soon. *What the fuck do I do now?* he thought.

2

David Wilson was the school idiot and was expelled more times than he would like to remember. He was a tall, lean boy with a gaunt face covered in spotty skin with thin, wispy brown hair cut short around his dreary face. He finally quit school and got a job at the local animal slaughterhouse in Hyde. David had been there over six years now, and he liked it as he didn't have to speak to anybody. David had no feelings when it came to animals and crushing their lifeless bones into a machine was rather soothing to him. David had no life apart from caring for his sick mother. His father had died long ago when he was a young boy, and he was an only child. It was just him and his mum now. They lived in a council house in Ashton and David caught the local bus to and from work each day. He would sit on the bus and watch the passengers, thinking what it might be like to be them. Anything to get his mind off his stinking life and the hopeless future he could foresee.

David's life changed dramatically one Saturday afternoon whilst he was out shopping on Ashton market. He wandered up and down the outdoor stalls that were lined in rows and offered a myriad of items including bedding, clothes, handbags, kitchen and electrical appliances. The merchandise was stacked high onto large wooden tables covered with colourful canvas to keep out the rain. One row of stalls was dedicated to the best fruit and vegetables found in Ashton. And at the best price. The storeowners would be shouting out their deals, bartering with the public, trying to pull in the passing crowds. David made his way through the crowds and entered the indoor market. This building was built in 1829 and is a true icon of the town. The large, red-bricked square building, along with the beautiful arched windows and decorative entrance stood out against the pale blue sky. Positioned on top of this grand building was the infamous clock tower, which held a large, black and white clock face on each of its four walls, that could be seen from anywhere in the local vicinity.

His mother had given him the weekly shopping list, and David was diligently ticking off the items as he acquired them in the indoor food section of the old market. He was just heading over to the cheese stand when he was accidentally pushed into the nearby entrance of a small bookstall. To steady himself, David grabbed onto an old wooden bookshelf which instantly collapsed sending countless books sprawling to the floor, along with his two shopping bags full of vegetables, bread, butter, bacon and milk. David felt so stupid and looked around to see who had pushed into him. 'Are you okay, lad?' said the man behind the counter. 'Bloody kids again, I keep telling the management they should not let those rascals in here, but they never listen to me,' he said. David smiled and began to pick up his supplies. The man knelt down and started to gather up the selection of books. David put his bags down and helped the man re-position them on their rightful shelves. 'No harm done, lad,' said the man. 'Why don't you pick yourself a book from there,' he said whilst pointing at the shelves. 'It'll be on the house, of course.' David was no avid reader, but he skimmed the books and something caught his eye. It was a large, black, leather-bound volume with the words *Occult* written on the sleeve. He opened the book and was drawn to the chapter titled *Spells to improve your life.*

'Thanks,' said David, 'I'll take this one if that's okay?' The man smiled, and David put the book into his bag and continued on with his shopping.

By the time he arrived home, David was feeling tired so he went into his room and lay on his bed. He was just drifting off to sleep when he remembered the book. He raced downstairs and found it on the kitchen table. David's life changed that day. The book disclosed conjuring spells for the novice to try. Spells that could evoke evil spirits to transform one's drab and often painful life. David longed for a different life one of wealth, pleasures and supremacy. He spent the whole weekend in his room, apart from making meals for his mother. On the following Monday after work, David stopped off at the markets and began to fill his bags with items from a list he compiled from the book. Candles, chalk, matches and steel containers. He managed to steal some animal bones from work and went to the local butcher shop for some offal.

Once tea had been made and the dishes cleared away, David retired to his room. He ripped up the old faded carpet that covered his room and began making strange markings on the wooden floorboards with the chalk. He kept returning to the book, following all instructions methodically. The ritual involved using some of his own blood with David slicing the inside of his arm carefully and catching the droplets of red liquid into a small metal bowl. He read out loud the incantations and positioned everything as directed. David sat on the floor and waited. At first, nothing happened. He lit a cigarette and then studied the book some more. He began to repeat the words over and over again, but it was no use, nothing happened. David threw the book across the room and got in bed.

He was just starting to drift off when he smelt a deathly stench coming from the centre of his bedroom. He sat up in bed and reached for his lamp positioned on a small wooden side table. As soon as he had clicked on the switch David could see a mass of blackness hovering around the circle David had drawn earlier on the wooden floor. He began to feel uneasy and lay down pulling the covers over his head. There was no sound coming from the blackness, but David could feel someone or something coming closer to his bed. 'Do not be afraid, David,' said a deep voice. David clenched his eyes shut and prayed the thing would go away. 'Come now, David, I mean you no harm; after all, it was you who summoned me here.' David could not believe his ears, what the fuck was happening here. *Had he really caused this thing to appear in his room?* he thought.

'What do you want?' said David shaking underneath the safety of his bed sheets.

'I want to thank you, David,' said the demon.

'For what?' replied David.

'You have freed me from a life of senseless purgatory where I had no one or nothing to do with my time except sit in darkness,' said the demon. 'I am contented to be amongst this Earth plane once more, and for that reason, David; I am here to show you my gratitude.' David tried to scream out but the sound would not come. He was frozen to the bed and could now see the

15

black vapour rising over him. 'Come, David, don't be shy, what is it you really want?' asked the demon.

'I want you to go away,' said David. 'I need some time to think.'

'Very well, David, I shall return in the morrow and you will give me your answer,' said the demon. David opened his eyes and peeped out from beneath the sheets. He saw the blackness disappear along with the stench as the air began to clear.

David got out of bed and picked up the book which had been thrown to the other side of the room. He studied it carefully and began reading about the summoning of a demon. He now realised what he had done, and David rushed to the bathroom and vomited in the sink. He went downstairs and got a drink of water and sat down at the kitchen table to steady his nerves. 'A fucking demon,' he kept saying, over and over again. David didn't get much sleep that night so the next morning he called in sick at work. After making his mother breakfast, David went back to his room. He had to think about what the demon has said. *What could this thing really do to help me?* he thought. *What is it I really want?* David hated his existence and longed for something to change. He loved his mother very much and wished that they had more money so he could get her all the help she needed. *That's it*, he thought. *Yes, I will ask for more money so I can look after my mum.* David waited all day for the demon to reappear, but nothing happened. That evening he laid awake with his bed covers close to hand in case the black thing hovered towards him, but again, there was nothing. In the morning David started to think he had dreamt about the demon and after kissing his mother goodbye, he left for his usual journey to work.

A few weeks went by, and David had almost forgotten about the book, and he had even replaced the old carpet back over the floorboards. Life was exactly the same; nothing had changed. He was running for the bus and missed it. *Fuck it,* he thought as he started to walk along the road. He went past a small pub which had just opened for the night, so he stepped inside. David was not much of a drinker, but it was better than waiting half an hour for the next bus. He ordered half a lager and sat down at a small table opposite the bar. The pub was empty apart from a few regulars. Soon the barmaid approached him and asked David if he was interested in filling out one of the local "Spot the Ball" entries. This was a weekly event where people were asked to draw an X in the exact location that a football had been in before it entered the net, scoring a goal. The odds were outlandish, but that didn't stop anybody from spending a few pounds having a go. The prize was two hundred and fifty thousand pounds, which was quite a lot of money in the 1980s. David could not resist and filled out one of the coupons. The barmaid entered it into the machine and David finished his beer, picked up the coupon and headed out the door.

It was not until the weekend that David found himself being the winner of that week's "Spot the Ball". His mother fainted when he told her the news and David didn't sleep for a week. They had to travel down to London to pick up the prize money, and David treated his mother to a holiday in the big City. Life was certainly on the up for David. He quit the meat factory, and they bought a huge house in Stalybridge overlooking the town. David hired professional carers for his mother and spent thousands on her medical bills. He bought himself a silver Porsche and a whole new wardrobe of clothes. With the money came the lifestyle. David soon had a string of so-called friends wanting to spend every second with him. His mother regained her health and was sent on a round the world cruise. It was as if everything David touched now turned to gold.

Several months later whilst David was resting on his large, expensive sofa, the room began to fill with a deathly odour. David sat up and surveyed the room quickly as he had no problem in remembering that stench. He reached for his smokes on the glass coffee table and lit a cigarette and inhaled. Before his very eyes, a black vessel of smoke-like vapour materialised, only a few inches from David's face. 'Are you pleased with your life now, David?' the demon said. 'Did I treat you well?' David coughed and almost choked on the smoke. It all came flooding back to him, the book and the strange encounter with the same voice that night in his bedroom.

'What do you want?' David shouted out.

'Come now, a deal is a deal, is it not?' replied the demon.

'Hang on a minute,' replied David. 'What do you mean about a deal?'

'You asked for my help and I gave it to you. Is your life not better?'

'Yes,' replied David still trying to make sense of what was happening.

'Very well, now is the time for you to do something for me,' said the voice.

David took another long drag of his cigarette before answering, 'What do you mean, I won that money on "Spot the Ball".'

'Come now, David, are you that stupid to think that you won that by chance?' said the demon chuckling out loud. 'You are not that fortunate.'

'You mean you made me win it,' replied David.

'Well, you asked for your life to be better, so I arranged it.'

'How can you do that sort of thing?' said David. He really did not believe the demon was telling him the truth, but he had no way of proving it wasn't him either. 'What do I have to do?' asked David with a suspicion that it wouldn't be something good.

Now the demon was very cunning and knew that David was not the most intelligent of his species, but nevertheless, the demon knew he had to be careful. He needed a body to possess so it would help him to navigate in this world. Once inside the vessel he would have full control over the body. He knew that the human's soul would be damned forever and the body completely destroyed. The demon also knew he could not enter the body without permission so he had to convince David that he would come to no harm. 'I need a vessel to use so I can walk amongst the living,' the demon replied. David had no idea who he was bargaining with. This demon could lie and manipulate in order to get what he wanted. David didn't know it, but his life would soon be over.

'You mean you want me as your vessel thing?' said David stubbing out his cigarette and placing another one in his mouth. His hands were shaking, and he knew he was in trouble.

'That is correct, David. I will enter you and use your body to explore this Earth plane.'

'What if I refuse?' said David.

'Why would you refuse me after all, haven't I brought you all that you wished for?' said the demon.

'Well, how long would you need my body for? And how will I know when you are in it?' asked David. The demon told David what he wanted to hear, that it would be painless; like David was sleeping. He forgot to mention that once the demon had David's body, he was not going to return it. 'What if I say no?' asked David again. 'Would you harm me?'

The demon continued to lie, 'I would not harm thee, I just need a vessel for a short time,' he said. 'I will ask permission before I enter thee and leave you unharmed.' David loved his new life and feared that the voice would take it all away. He trusted the demon's words and sadly gave permission for the thing to enter his body. The black venomous vapour that had been swirling in front of David suddenly rushed into his mouth. David's whole body became stiff, and he fell back onto the sofa. His eyes opened wide and rolled up inside his head. When they returned, blackness had poured over them, and David was no more.

3

'Come on, Beth! It's eight o'clock, we're going now, and you will be late for college, see you later love,' yelled Beth's mum as she and her husband left for work.

Two skinny arms appeared out of the bedspread and stretched out into the cold air. Meanwhile snuggled up close to Beth was Tina, the family's much-loved black and grey miniature poodle. 'Come on, Tina, move yourself, we have to get up, or I will be late again.' Beth Cotten threw the warm covers back and Tina, with much reluctance, jumped down and waited for her master. Beth quickly grabbed her dressing gown and started off down the carpeted stairs and opened the communal front door. She shivered as Tina ran outside and found her favourite spot on the lawn, 'Hurry up, sweetheart, I'm freezing out here,' said Beth wrapping her knee-length robe around her trim body even tighter. It was September with most mornings and evenings full of crisp, cool temperatures.

Beth and her parents had been living in the top flat for two years now. Mr and Mrs Rothers, both in their eighties, had converted their large, semi-detached house into two flats with the Rothers occupying the downstairs part of the house (Flat 1) and Beth's parents residing upstairs (Flat 2). It had two bedrooms, a large living room and generous kitchen and bathroom. The semi-detached property was positioned in over an acre of land and well set back from the main road. Beth's mum had redecorated the flat with lush, pale green carpets and antique white painted walls. The kitchen had all the "mod cons", and the bathroom was tiled from floor to ceiling with large, glossy, white tiles with a *posh* basin and glass shower door. Beth thought it was very trendy for a flat in the early 1980s and she loved living there. The Rothers were lovely, caring people and the two pensioners and the Cotten family had become the best of friends.

Beth quickly raced Tina back up the stairs and into the kitchen. She clumsily poured Tina's dog biscuits into a bowl and ran into the bathroom for a marathon shower. Beth quickly dried herself off, stepping into a pair of blue denim jeans and slipped on a yellow T-shirt. Looking in the mirror, the reflection showed a young girl, 18 years old, with pretty features, big blue eyes and ivory skin. Her shoulder-length hair was a huge mass of natural chestnut brown curls, and her smile showed a perfect set of white teeth. Beth was about 5 feet 2 inches with a slim build and curved figure. She sat on the bed and pulled on her favourite blue ankle boots, as she grabbed her red leather motorcycle jacket. She picked up her canvas bag, which was slumped in the same position it had been thrown in the day before. 'Give me a kiss sweetheart,' Beth said as Tina bounced into her arms and licked her face. 'See you tonight and be a good girl,' Beth darted down the stairs and walked up the long paved driveway turning left onto Junction Street. She walked under the old stone railway bridge heading towards Victoria Road, where she would wait for the number 330 bus to take her into Ashton town centre. Along the way, Beth pulled out her portable Walkman with earphones and listened to AC/DC on full volume.

Beth walked into the large college art room at 9.15 am and looked around for a space on the floor. 'Oh good of you to join us, Beth,' said Mr Collins, he was the head of art at the Beaufort Road College.

'Sorry I am late, Mr Collins, I missed the bus,' said Beth with her head down. She hated being late but just couldn't seem to get to places on time, no matter how hard she tried. Her dad said she was always running on Beth's time!

'Seeing as you are here now you might as well take a spot on the floor and listen to the art project you will be doing this morning,' Mr Collins replied. He was a tall, lean man, about 50 years of age, which probably seemed ancient to this young bunch of teenagers, with greying hair and matching beard. He looked like an artist wearing a trendy black T-shirt and blue jeans. Mr Collins went outside and returned wheeling in an old pushbike which he turned upside down and laid it on its handlebars on top of a large table in the centre of the room. He went on to explain the art project for the day stating that each student was to create a semi-abstract collage using only one colour and black and white. There was a huge array of bright coloured papers on the floor with a selection of paints, coloured charcoal, oil pastels and art equipment including brushes, water pots and empty paint trays.

Beth grabbed her choice of coloured paper (orange) and various art mediums and began sketching parts of the bicycle. Beth was in her element, ever since her big sister Gail had given her a box of poster paints and brushes when she was about seven, Beth had been in love with painting and drawing. She had won many art competitions and all of her teachers proclaimed, 'Beth has a real talent.' Her goal was to complete this foundation course and study fine art at a more prestigious art school in London. Beth was the youngest of four and was the only child remaining at home. Her big sister Gail, ten years older than Beth, left the family home when she was seventeen and was pregnant by the time Beth turned eight. Her two older brothers had joined the forces and were both married. Beth's mum and dad were hard working. Her mum managed a women's coat stall in Hyde Market, and Beth's father had done numerous work, mostly manual and was now working for the local council maintaining the streetlights in the town and neighbouring roads. They both adored Beth, and she loved them both very much. They were supportive of her career in the arts and only wanted Beth to be happy. Her parents may have worked hard but they also knew how to enjoy themselves and you could find them both in the local pub each night, bringing fish and chip supers home for Beth to *dig in* with them. Beth's life was perfect, and she had big plans for her future.

As soon as morning tea break was announced, Beth ran for the entrance and looked around for her best friend. Emily was a little taller than Beth with short, straight brown hair. She was attractive, however; her nose was rather prominent, and she had more weight on her hips and thighs. Emily knew how to dress and wore outrageous clothes. Today she was wearing bright green pants and a loose white blouse that draped down to her knees. A flowered headband covered her hair, and she wore large, silver looped earrings. 'Beth, have you got any ciggies?' Emily asked.

'Sure do,' said Beth tucking into her canvas bag pulling out a packet of Benson and Edges. The two chatted about the project until the subject of Friday night came up. 'I can't wait for the weekend, Em,' Beth said with the hugest smile on her face.

'I wonder why,' laughed Emily. Beth and Emily, along with a bunch of other girls met each weekend at the local rock pub named "The Dog and Hound" in Stalybridge, where they enjoyed watching live bands. They would then *cadge* rides from various guys on their motorbikes and end the night at a rock club in Manchester.

Jenny only lived a couple of streets down from Beth, and even though they had only known each other for the past twelve months or so, Beth and Jenny had become the best of friends. They met in a local pub where Jenny was working behind the bar. She was the same height as Beth but struggled with her weight. Her hair was cut short to her head, and Jenny had the biggest, rosiest cheeks and a cheesy grin. Beth and Jenny spent most weekends catching the train together and having fun at the rock clubs in the city. Jenny had three sisters, and Beth loved staying at her house in the top bunk of Jenny's bed. They would catch the late bus home from Manchester, and it was safer for Beth to sleep at Jenny's place, so she didn't have to walk the last few streets alone.

Beth had a huge crush on the bass player of a local rock band named "Fire", and she wanted to talk with him, but her nerves always got in the way. Beth never had any trouble "copping off" with boys at the rock clubs, however; in Beth's eyes, none of them was like Jake; he was the very definition of cool. Jake was over six feet tall, with a lean body and a head full of lavish black hair that fell perfectly right down to his waist. He had a black moustache and wore all black clothing including a cool leather biker's jacket. He had an unusual similarity to a young Christopher Lee! Beth was totally besotted by him and went to jelly whenever he was around. The girls laughed about this all the time, but Beth secretly pained for the opportunity to talk to Jake and hoped he would be at the pub this Friday. If not, she definitely knew that he would be there next weekend, as his band were playing at the Dog and Hound; the girls' local. Beth knew she would have to arrange to get the girls there early so they could grab the table nearest to the stage, so Jake would have no option but to look at her.

As soon as the girls had finished their cigarettes, it was time to recommence work on their pending masterpiece. The morning flew by, and lunch was spent with a small group in the local pub where they devoured a chicken burger and glass of coca cola. The afternoon found the girls studying sculpture where they were assigned to small groups and were asked to create paper sculptures. Three o'clock arrived and the girls walked together down Beaufort Road into Ashton bus station, chatting about what they would wear on the weekend and who they fancied. 'See you tomorrow, gorgeous,' said Emily as she ran for her bus.

'Be good, Em,' Beth replied as she waited in line for the 330 to arrive.

Beth arrived home to greet her dad who was driving up the pathway. Mr and Mrs Rothers opened the front door and smiled with affection. 'Hello, Beth, did you have a good day at college?' asked Mrs Rothers.

'Oh yes, thanks I did,' replied Beth and gave the most beautiful smile.

'You won't forget us will you love, when you become a famous artist,' said Mr Rothers. All three of them began to giggle.

'Good afternoon, James,' said Mr Rothers to Beth's dad who had just parked his car. 'How was your day?'

James smiled and replied, 'Too long,' and gave a chuckle.

They chatted for a while then Beth and her dad made their way up the stairs greeted ecstatically by Tina, who of course was so pleased to see them. 'Hello, girl! How have you been?' said Beth.

'I think someone needs a walk,' said James with Beth reaching for Tina's lead.

'I'm already on it, Dad,' she said.

Tina and Beth walked down Junction Street under the railway bridge and through to Victoria Road. Tina stopped to sniff as many pieces of grass as she could before Beth would grow impatient and pull on her lead. Beth lit up a cigarette and took in the local scenery. Most people were still at work, so the road was not that busy. The day had been dry, so there were no nasty puddles to watch out for. There were no houses on this stretch of the road just industrial areas where large ugly brickwork shot out of the ground with thin chimneys blowing grey smoke into the already grey sky above. Large, unattractive steel gates kept unwanted visitors out. There was a café nearer to Victoria Road where all the workers would meet for their traditional egg and bacon "sarnie" and burgers at lunch. The shop was empty at this time with the staff busy cleaning the outside tables and stacking the chairs. Beth and Tina turned around and began their stroll back home. When they were back in the warmth, Beth and Tina dived on the sofa. They both fell asleep with Tina tucked in next to Beth's stomach with Beth's arms cuddled around her.

At five o'clock, James woke Beth and asked if she wanted to go for a ride to pick up Mum. Beth always liked driving with her dad, so she jumped off the sofa and headed for the stairs. Tina of course was allowed on this particular outing as Mum loved it when Tina came along. They drove up Cheetham Hill Road and then onto Ashton Road, which leads into the centre of Hyde. They parked the car and walked through the outside market where most traders were packing up the contents of their stalls, ready for another day. There was a cold wind blowing through the market, and most people were hurrying to get back to the comfort of their own homes. They soon arrived at the entrance to the indoor part of the shopping mall and the coat stall was at the entrance on the right. It was small and cluttered with racks of women's coats. There was a large mirror where women could try on their wares and view how they fitted. Beth's mum was finishing up the takings of the day. 'Hi, Mum,' said Beth. 'We're here to take you home.'

'Oh, that is good news,' Jane replied, 'I'm about done for the day.'

'Have you been busy, love?' said James as he came into the store.

'So-so' was the reply. Jane's eyes lit up when she saw Tina stroll in behind James and she swooped down and picked her up. 'Well, how's my baby then?' Jane said while she gave Tina a big kiss.

'Come on, love, shut the shop so we can get home and have something to eat, I'm starving.' Jane switched off the lights and locked the door.

Jane's friend Annie, who owned the flower stall at the entrance, greeted Beth and James with a smile. 'Yes, take this poor woman home, James, she has worked hard today.'

'Only today!' said James, winking at his wife.

'See you tomorrow, Annie,' Jane said as they were leaving.

'You sure will honey, have a good night.'

'What shall we have for tea?' said Jane.

'What about some fresh turkey and rolls from the bakers,' replied Beth, 'I love those.'

Both parents nodded, and James said, 'Some chips would go nice with that, love,' as he turned towards Jane.

'Chips it is then,' Jane said, and all three laughed. Jane called into the bakery and ordered six fresh floury muffins and a huge handful of fresh turkey. They arrived home, and Jane went straight into the kitchen to prepare the meal. Beth set the table while James watched the local news on the television. After the feast, Jane and James retired to the bedroom for a nap, while Beth and Tina resumed their positions on the sofa. Around seven o'clock, the parents could be heard getting ready in the bathroom as they prepared for their night out at the local pub. 'See you later, love,' called James as they both went down the stairs towards the front door.

'See you later,' replied Beth.

Beth watched television and left the sofa once to get a drink and made a quick telephone call to Jenny. They discussed their plans for Friday night, and it was arranged that they would meet at the local bus stop to begin their night out. At ten thirty, James and Jane arrived back at the house with fresh fish and chips and two of their special friends Joyce and Gary. The couple were in their late fifties, and both worked at the local cigarette factory across the road from Beth's house. Joyce and Gary were friendly and loved to have a laugh. They had been friends for a long time. 'Want some fish and chips?' asked Joyce.

Beth was already in her pyjamas but smiled and said, 'Yes, please.' They all *pigged out* with fresh bread and butter, and Beth made a chip *butty* that she gulped down in record time. Beth left the couples reminiscing and said goodnight. She led Tina outside to empty her bladder on the lawn and soon they were both safely amongst the covers and snoring!

4

At six am, just as the sun was rising on a dim September Sunday morning, Brian Middleton stepped outside Number 1 Cedar Lane. It was a crisp 8 centigrade, and he wore appropriate clothes to safeguard against the cold. He was around 5 feet 10 inches, a stocky man with a slight bulging at his midriff. His clothes were of the finest, even for his medial gardening tasks, and included freshly ironed blue denim jeans, navy crew neck woollen jumper, topped off with an olive knee-length Barbour Long Hurst wax jacket with soft checked lining and fur-lined collar. His wellingtons were, of course, Barbour and black with a tartan lining. Brian's hair was thinning on top and covering his small dark brown, almost black eyes, were a pair of designer glasses with thick, acrylic black frames. His eyesight had always been less than average, and he had noticed it slowly diminishing over the years through years of scrutinising small print, mostly numbers, as he was an accountant for a large family firm in Manchester.

He closed the white front door of his red brick bungalow and walked down the paved pathway from his house, which was hemmed with a black metal fence. Number 1 Cedar Lane was accompanied by three other identical bungalows each set out in a row. The street was safely tucked away from the main road, and as the street progressed, an array of wooden and metal garages took their place. Brian strolled across the quiet road heading for the large allotment that took up most of the opposite side of the street. The allotment space was sectioned off into various sizes of land and nestled amongst the land were small wooden sheds where each gardener would diligently attend to potting seedlings and store his/her gardening equipment. Brian had one of the largest allotment spaces, which spread vertically almost in a straight line from one end of the allotment to the other. His shed was located closer to the road and on the right-hand side.

Gardening was not one of the pass times one would usually associate with a serial killer, but nonetheless, Brian enjoyed many pursuits which included his essential ingredient of seclusion. Apart from the odd old person attending to their garden, Brian enjoyed the luxury of isolation, especially when he was inside his shed. He had spent many dedicated hours arranging his small sanctuary which housed an array of comforts including a kettle, to make his selection of hot beverages on a cold day, a record player and cassette player to listen to a selection of classical music whenever the need arose. There was a small bar fridge stocked with beers and snacks, a large comfy armchair and desk that was surrounded by shelves of pot plants, garden equipment and gardening manuals. At the rear end of the shed was a large wooden table filled with a selection of seedlings that had been potted including turnips, spinach and other oriental vegetables.

To look at Brian, one would not see anything out of the ordinary. Brian was an only child and never knew his father. His mother said, 'The bastard died before you were born.' It turned out Brian was the result of a one-night stand when his mother was intoxicated at a party. His mother was of average height and had a slender figure. She wore the most expensive clothes, usually black, and glittering jewellery. Although her makeup was always flawless, it could not conceal the harshness of her face and clenched mouth. Her hair was short and styled every week at the local hairdressers, along with her nails, which were painted bright red. Brian's memory of his mother was poor but he never forgot her red shiny nails. Although his mother never beat him, there was an element of psychological abuse with his mother totally abandoning him emotionally from the day he was born.

His mother came from a very wealthy family and shame of the pregnancy nearly ruined her. She was well educated, and her parents had great expectations of their only daughter taking over the large agricultural business which had been handed down throughout previous generations. Brian remembered being abused by his mother on regular occasions and he was never allowed down at dinner to sit with the family. He often ate his meals, prepared in advance by the cook, in his bedroom feeling miserable and all alone. He could not understand why his mother was so cruel to him. All he ever wanted was to be loved by her.

As soon as Brian was old enough he was sent away to boarding school. There he became subjected to even more abuse by the older boys at the school. He gained weight, and this brought on uglier name-calling and being chased around the school gardens until he collapsed from lack of oxygen. 'Get up you fat pig,' the older boys would shout. 'You are a disgusting pig and you know what happens to pigs don't you?' Brian's life went from misery to more despair each day. There was no escaping the bullies as most of the boys bordered at the accommodation on the premises. His room was often ransacked and his clothes smothered in shit. It was no use trying to tell anyone, as this only resulted in more abuse. He was allowed home in the holidays but never saw his mother.

By the time Brian was nine years of age both his grandparents had passed away, and his mother was travelling in Europe spending the family inheritance as fast as she could. She developed a gambling problem and became a cocaine addict. Brian was taken care of by the domestic staff at the large six bedroomed home outside Chester. He never really knew why his mother hated him so much. By the time he was graduating from high school the family home had been repossessed by creditors. All the graceful furniture, trimmings and family jewellery were sold to pay out the debts his mother had quickly acquired. The staff lost their jobs, and Brian was left to fend for himself. Luckily his mind was sharp, and he had earned a scholarship to study accountancy. Brian found himself a part-time job and studied hard at Manchester University. His mother never contacted him again. He didn't even know if she was dead, but he suspected she would be with all the drinking and drugs. In any case, Brian was devoid of any feelings for his mother; they were blocked out years ago.

As he matured and went onto university Brian discovered that his intelligence could work in his favour. Brian was an expert at superficial charm, and although he could not feel any emotions, he soon learned how to mimic social etiquette and mannerisms to help him get by. Brian met his wife Ava Babitch while they were at university. Ava was from Croatia, one of the former republics of Yugoslavia. She grew up on a farm in Slavonia, the inland part of this country where the winters are very cold with hot, humid summers. Her parents both worked the land on their family farm and sent Ava off to school to gain an education. Ava studied hard and gained entrance to the University of Manchester where she studied chemistry and pharmacology. This is where the couple met back in 1955, and they married in 1960 when both Ava and Brian were twenty-five years old.

She was now in her mid-forties and time had not been kind to Ava. She was only five-foot-tall with excess weight now clinging to her hips and midriff. Her hair was short, greying, and had lost its natural shine. She had never been a beauty even back in the 1960s with plain looks, large nose and chin, which now seemed to be exaggerated as she grew older. Ava was a quiet and timid person, which suited Brian perfectly. He was able to charm her with his fake charismatic personality while deep down he had no concern for anyone or anything. He realised early that he needed someone to wash his clothes and cook his meals and Ava seemed interested, so that made him apply some effort in order to acquire her services. He had never really been into the sex thing with her although when they were younger, he remembered wanting it more often. These days the couple slept in separate rooms, as Brian had grown accustomed to sleeping by himself for the past twenty years or so. He stated that it was because of his snoring and that he didn't want to disturb Ava while she slept. Ava could not care less as she was quite content to be left alone. On the odd occasion Brian felt horny, he would summon Ava into his bed, and when the act was over, she would be immediately directed back to her own room.

There were certain occasions where Brian would show some affection towards Ava especially on her birthday or at Christmas, as Brian was no fool and he realised the importance of showing some appreciation for her, as he did not want her poisoning him or worse—even thinking of leaving him. He had grown very accustomed to his lifestyle, and Ava was exceptional at keeping his surroundings in immaculate condition. Ava's parents were both deceased, and she had no other family to speak of left living. This was how Brian liked it—no nosey, interfering family to try and disturb his equilibrium. Ava found herself alone in this strange country which had now become her home. She had learned the English language well, however; she still spoke with a strong accent. There was no pitter-patter of tiny feet in this home, as Brian had forbidden Ava from even thinking about having children. She was ordered to have her "tubes tied" as soon as the couple married. Ava, being the submissive young girl at the time, agreed and the deed was done. She worked at a local chemist shop which helped relieve the monotony of her married life. Brian was very obsessive and dictated how and where she could go for most of the time. She had no real friends—only her colleagues at work, which she was very grateful for. Her only true escape was each Sunday morning when she was allowed to go to the local church. Brian hated religion and those memories of being dragged to church by his mother. He had no interest in accompanying Ava on Sundays, however; he did allow her to leave the house on these occasions.

Brian entered the allotment gate and gazed delightedly at his plot which was by far the most exquisite and superior of all the gardens on this particular site. What was immediately apparent was the long, thick line of colourful perennial flowers including the bright purple Salvia with silvery green leaves and small, delicate violet flowers held on long purple stems. There were Penstemons with elegant, lance-shaped leaves and a burst of crimson red flowers nestled next to bright yellow Chrysanthemums and pure white Peonies. In front of the flowers were onions, potatoes, leeks, courgettes and tomatoes, all ready for harvesting. Today, Brian would be collecting his bounty of produce to give to his wife, ready for making the food Brian was accustomed to. Ava would turn the vegetables into winter soups and stews accompanied by her homemade bread. She had become very proficient at baking and cooking as it was important to keep her husband happy. Brian had a tendency for getting nasty with her if she served him a meal he did not like.

Ava did have one close friend at work, Angela, and the pair would giggle together at lunchtime and often walk home together as Angela lived only a few streets away from Ava. Angela was a few years younger than Ava and lived with her older sister. She had been married once although that seemed an eternity ago. Her husband died unexpectedly from a heart attack a few years ago. Since that time, Angela had found comfort living with her sister

Anne. Angela worked at the front counter of the chemist shop and although her schooling did not match up to Ava's qualifications, nor did her level of intelligence, the two women seemed to hit it off straight away. Ava would not dare tell Brian of her friendship, as there was no way of knowing how he would take it out on her, and Ava did not want to take that chance. Angela knew that Ava was very unhappy yet Ava would go all strange if the subject was approached. 'I am doing okay, Angela,' she would say, and Angela would always leave it at that. They would quickly resume their giggling looking at the array of fashion and celebrity magazines found in the tea room at the back of the shop. Angela smoked and Ava would often accompany her outside the building where Angela would give a full account of her dating mishaps and troubles with her grown-up kids. Ava loved every minute of this as being at home with Brian was like living in a stuffy old library, the kind Ava had spent many years roaming around whilst at university. There was hardly any noise in their home, apart from the TV or Brian's morbid music, which he played often, and if there ever was a conversation between the two, Brian would say his piece and leave Ava before she even got the chance to have her say. Ava's life was purgatory, and she felt trapped. Ava longed for the day when she could escape, however; she was too frightened and where would she go?

Brian stepped inside his long-standing, musty, wooden shed and flicked the humble light switch. He put the kettle on and switched on a small electric heater to break through the damp cold air. He settled down in his comfy armchair and pressed start on his cassette tape player. Ah! His favourite piece of music was about to commence, and Brian laid his head back, closed his eyes and revelled in the darkness of the sounds. The *Rite of Spring* composed by the infamous Russian Igor Stravinsky. Apparently, the sounds caused quite a stir when it was first performed within Diaghilev's ballet company back in Paris in 1913, with its acclaimed avant-garde nature causing a near riot in the audience. This particular piece of music appealed to Brian, not only for the powerful and shocking sounds it expressed but for the concept, this was what truly attracted him, and although there is no telling when this man began his killing of women, or how many poor young females had fallen victim to this monster, the concept is eerily disturbing, and what's more, it becomes even more horrific when a serial killer makes it part of his own reality.

The story behind the music portrays a celebration of spring, with young girls arriving from the hilltops assembling at the foot of the river where they begin to dance the *Dance of Abduction* amongst the wise elders headed by the Sage who commands the ritual games and blessings of the Earth. Brian listens to the melodies brought to life by a solo bassoon, eagerly joined by voluminous woodwind instruments and eventually combined by strings. Listening to the music Brian is almost in a trance state. He sees himself as the wise Sage and in command of the procession, the people break into a passionate dance becoming one with the Earth. In come the brass and percussion instruments stirring Brian to an almost frenzy, as he grows impatient waiting for Part II, the sacrifice. Brian's heart begins to quicken, thinking of the fair young girls each engaging in mysterious games and dances. The *la piece de resistance* signifying the honourable chosen one! One of the maidens is chosen by fate for the sacrificial offering to the pagan gods. The girl then dances to her death. The music is violent, loud and the large percussion instruments are given full voice, conveying rhythmic power and such cruelty. Brian is fully emerging into his fantasy. Soon he would be planning and stalking his next innocent victim.

5

Harry swung open the large wooden doors to the community centre and entered. The familiar old musty smell greeted him along with scented candles and the noisy chatter of a large group of people, some sitting, others standing around in small groups. He walked briskly past the small wooden table at the entrance which had raffle tickets and a basket of goodies portrayed on it and squeezed himself through a small opening in a large circle of grey plastic chairs. He then approached a large altar table covered in pure white cloth flowing to the wooden floor, with beautifully lit candles on top and was met by Reverend Elizabeth. 'Harry, welcome my love; so glad you could make it.' Harry's eyes widened, and he smiled as he sat down beside her. The crowd grew larger with people bustling into the old community building finding seats as they arrived. There were book stalls and crystal jewellery stalls ladened around the hall, and at the back of the premises was a small kitchen with two large ladies making sandwiches and carrying out plates of chocolate cake and assorted buns and biscuits, ready for the get-together after the service.

At 7 pm sharp the community doors were shut tight and the service began with Reverend Elizabeth welcoming everyone and giving her usual prayer. 'I would like to introduce everybody to our special guest tonight, Mr Harry O Neal, who is one of the best psychics I know.' Harry blushed. The reverend went on, 'He travels around the country giving readings and he also works with the local police. Please put your hands together for Harry.' The crowd, now over fifty people, sat around in the semi-circle, stood up and clapped. Harry found himself standing up and heading for the centre of the circle. He was a tall, lean man around thirty-five years of age with a full head of auburn hair which was shoulder-length and spiked on top. He had pronounced cheekbones and a large Roman nose with a dimpled and protruding chin and sparkling brown eyes. Harry wore a long ankle-length brown coat which covered his blue jeans and concealed a white cotton shirt that he wore underneath. On his feet, he wore black and white sneakers; a kind of David Tenant look about him if one was to compare.

Harry closed his eyes, and the lights were dimmed. He took three long deep breaths and cleared his mind of any distracting thoughts. He felt the temperature rise and could feel the energy in the room which was a mixture of anticipation and at the same time, a beautiful feeling of adoration. Harry looked into his mind's eye and saw clearly a young boy who was around seven years of age wearing blue knee-length shorts and a white T-shirt with dinosaurs on the front. The boy's hair was golden brown, and his eyes were the truest blue. The boy was at the roadside and seemed to be turning his head sideways left and right looking at the traffic to see if it was clear for him to cross the busy road. Harry sensed that the boy was nervous and hesitant in making the crossing, however; the boy was intent on getting his red ball which had rolled across the pavement and was now at the other side of the tarmacked road. Cars rushed by, and the boy became flustered and made a run for it to retrieve his toy. Harry felt a pain in his head so fierce that he had to put his hand up to his face. He became pale and felt nauseous instantly. The next image Harry saw was of the boy's small body lying distorted on the cold black surface of the road. There were people shouting and screaming as the traffic ceased to a halt with someone running over to cover the boy's now limp body with their coat. Harry began to breathe heavily and felt dizziness overtake his body. His legs began to buckle underneath his weight, so he quickly sat down on the cold wooden floor. No one said a word in the hall that night as they watched Harry try to compose himself.

Suddenly Harry's vision in his mind changed to the small boy who was now smiling at him, and Harry felt a great sense of relief. The boy began to speak in a soft child-like manner. 'Hey mister, I'm Tim, I'm okay now, and I want you to let my mum and dad know and my big sister Annabel too.'

Harry smiled and spoke to the boy internally, 'You gave me quite a shock there, Tim, and I am glad that you are okay now. What is your mum's name, Tim?'

The boy replied with, 'Mary, Mary Doyle.'

'Is your mum here tonight in the hall?' asked Harry.

'Yep, she is there with the red top on and my sister Annabel is there with her.' Harry looked over at the crowd of people sitting around the circle, and he spotted Mary who was nervously looking in Harry's direction. He could see the anguish on Mary's face and the dark rings under her eyes which showed the agony this woman had been going through each night.

Harry spoke to Tim once more, 'What else would you like your family to know?'

'I want them to know that it didn't hurt, I am with my grandpa George who is really a lot of fun,' Tim smiled again as he replied.

Harry had a thought and asked Tim if he could wait a moment while Harry spoke to his mum. Tim eagerly nodded his head, and Harry stood up and walked slowly over to where Mary and her daughter were seated. Harry spoke in a soft tone, 'I have someone very special who wants to talk to you, Mary,' he said while kneeling down next to her.

Mary instantly burst into tears holding Annabel's hand tightly. 'Timmy, is it really Timmy?' she cried.

Harry motioned closer to her and put his arm around her. 'Yes, it really is Tim; he would like to tell you that he is all right and not to worry.'

Mary's tears ceased, and she looked into Harry's kind eyes, 'Where is he? And who is looking after him?' she replied.

Harry spoke to Tim who told him that his grandpa George and lots of other kind people were now looking after him. Harry relayed the message to his mother and witnessed some of her pain appearing to lift gradually from her face. Harry knew that this was a very important moment for both Tim and his family, where they could get the opportunity to say their goodbyes, but he knew time was short. 'Mary, is there something you would like to say to your Tim before he goes?'

Mary's tears began to flood down her cheeks as she strained to get the words out. 'I love you little man and always will, Tim, I am sorry I could not protect you and that you had to leave us all so soon. I want you to always remember how much we love you and that you will always be with us every single day.'

Harry asked Tim if he could hear his mother and Tim nodded with affection. 'What do you want to say to your mum and sister, Tim? While you can,' said Harry.

'I love you Mummy and my daddy and my Annabel, I am okay now and I don't want you to be sad anymore.' Harry conveyed Tim's sweet message and said goodbye to the little boy whose image began to fade in his mind.

Harry spent a further thirty minutes in the centre of that room giving what messages he could to other loved ones waiting to hear from their family members who had passed over. At the end of the session, the crowd gratefully thanked Harry, and the lights were raised and the evening concluded with a prayer. Harry found himself wanting to escape the attention, so he nipped outside for a smoke. Reverend Elizabeth followed him outside to check on him and found Harry perched on a small brick wall outside the main entrance. His head was down, and she knew he was struggling with something. 'Hey, Mr O Neal, you were great in there tonight,' she said.

Harry looked up briefly and tried to force a smile but really he felt like shit. 'I stuffed that whole thing up, Elizabeth, I was so shit. That poor mother, having to do that in front of all those fucking strangers, I should have taken her outside or something.'

Reverend Elizabeth smiled and took Harry's hand in hers and said, 'Harry, you really don't know, do you?' Harry looked up again into her eyes and she continued, 'You just gave that woman something so special that you don't even realise. She got the chance to say goodbye to her little boy and know that he is safe with his grandpa. It sucks I know that he had to go, but we have no control over that, only God does. Harry, my love, you need to see past the pain and focus on what you can offer these poor souls in terms of offering them some closure and hope.'

Harry sat up and inhaled his cigarette and finally smiled, 'I know you're right, Elizabeth, but it's fucking hard sometimes you know.'

'Yeah, I do know, Harry,' she said, 'but what choice do we have? We have been given these gifts, and it's up to us to work out how to use them without taking on all the woes of this world.' The two of them sat on the wall for a while and stared up into the night sky.

If you would have told Harry some years back that he would be spending his time working for the local police, using his psychic abilities, to help catch murderers or find missing persons for that matter and travelling around the country giving readings to all kinds of people about their dead loved ones, Harry would have laughed in your face. For his life had been truly mapped out according to his very wealthy parents. Harry was the youngest of three boys all of which, including Harry had been prepped to follow in the footsteps of their renowned father Dr Ian O Neal. Harry's older brothers Alec and David were both practising doctors each specialising in their own fields of paediatrics and gynaecology. Harry followed suit after graduating from Hyde grammar school and was sent off to study medicine at Liverpool University. It was there that Harry experienced a severe nervous breakdown and found himself recuperating at his parents' large home on Mottram Road in Stalybridge. This was all over ten years ago, and it had taken Harry many years to overcome his depression and finally figure out what he wanted to do with his life. That's when he met Reverend Elizabeth at one of his local meditation events, which had been helping Harry to come off the antidepressant medication. Harry didn't like the way he felt on the medication and searched for other methods of natural healing. The reverend, or *Rev* as Harry liked to call her, became his mentor and she introduced Harry to various healing experiences.

Harry had developed several psychic abilities including mediumship where he could communicate with spirits. Harry's ability came from within, and he would often see images in his mind's eye and hear information by auditory means. He also had the gift of clairsentience where Harry would be able to acquire information from objects and places. This was particularly useful when working with the police on a missing person's case. Harry would be able to touch a personal object that belonged to the person who had disappeared, and this would sometimes offer Harry images of places to search or people to contact.

Harry said his goodbyes to the Rev and walked over to his little blue Mini in the car park. He fastened his seat belt, turned on his radio and headed home. He had been living in Hyde for the past five years, as he worked at the local police station. Harry soon arrived home, letting himself into the warm unit on the outskirts of the small town. His big, furry, Persian cat Oliver greeted him at the door, and Harry went straight into the small kitchen to feed the hungry feline. Harry's living area was furnished elegantly with neutral-toned walls, soft carpet and furnishings. There were several wooden bookcases brimming with spiritualistic literature including new age topics, parapsychology, healings, military intelligence and paranormal activities. Harry also had a deep passion for art and music with his acoustic guitar propped over one of his armchairs and Harry's vinyl record collection stacked neatly near the record player. Harry kicked off his sneakers and spread himself across the couch. He drifted off into a deep sleep with Oliver settling down on his chest, and the pair slept well into the night.

6

The demon had succeeded in possessing a human body. It had been centuries in human time since he had visited this plane. He had been banished from heaven along with all the other fallen angels. That seemed too long ago to even remember now. The demon had existed in the lower levels of the astral planes spending the time in mischief and constructing his grand plan. He hated mankind and God, and; his only purpose was to wreak havoc and destruction against his God and recruit all who would follow him.

He knew he could not do this alone and he would need helpers, and the demon knew where such souls could be found. He left the house and made his way towards the local graveyard. Here he would be looking for ghosts of human beings who walked around on the Earth plane unaware of the passage of time. These poor souls were either found on the lower levels of the astral planes or stuck on the Earth plane lost to wander aimlessly for all eternity. They were not condemned to hell, and generally, they were not evil in nature, but the demon knew they were vulnerable and easy prey, as all they really wanted was to pass over into the light and put an end to their senseless existence.

The demon met no obstacle as he walked down Mottram Road, turning left into Armadale and eventually finding his way to the entrance of the cemetery on Hall Green Road. The body was difficult to manoeuvre at first, but as the demon became more comfortable with the strangeness of being inside a body again, the process became easier. Dukinfield Cemetery was opened in 1866 and was positioned overlooking the town. On a clear day, one can see as far as Saddle Worth and the green hillsides of the Yorkshire Moors. The demon strolled amongst the graves and sat quietly waiting for the sun to go down. The old graveyard was well tendered with the grass neatly mowed and weeds removed. There were colourful flowers carefully placed at loved one's graves, and the birds sang softly in the row of trees that fenced off this world of the dead from the living.

At dusk, he pulled himself up and began to walk around the old headstones. It wasn't long before he saw a young woman dressed in black sitting next to a large stone sculpture of an angel. The words encrypted below the angel read: *In loving memory of Scarlet Haines, loving daughter, wife and mother 1850-1875.* The demon approached and beckoned her to stand. The woman was of an era long gone, and her tattered clothes showed remnants of a long ankle-length skirt and a fitted blouse. Her hair had once been neatly tied up but now hung loosely around her grey gaunt face holding two sunken black eyes. A large gaping hole was showing in the side of her face where the skull bone peered through. 'My dear, come with me, I shall see thee home,' said the demon as he smiled. The women did not speak, and her thin, lifeless body followed the demon as he began to walk away. He soon found others needlessly moving around in the dark. The demon led them to a large tree where they stood surrounding him. The moon hovered overhead with its gentle streams of light falling on the deathless faces below. The demon promised them all freedom and a safe return to heaven. In return, he would require their assistance in all things evil. There was no resistance. They were to be his eyes and ears in the local vicinity. Watching and waiting for anyone or anything that may help the demon with his plan.

7

Beth entered the *Dog and Hounds* and scanned the place quickly. The pub had one long room with a large bar that stretched out from one end of the venue to the other. At the back of the room was a small wooden stage where live bands played on the weekends and Thursday nights. Chairs and small square tables were placed around the edges of the room with some already occupied. In a room to the left were a large pool table and a dartboard hung on the smoked stained wall. Small wooden tables were positioned against the interior walls. The toilets were at the back of the pub. Beth walked in slowly and recognised a few of the local guys wearing jeans, with their long hair flowing down their backs. Lynyrd Skynyrd was being played loudly by the DJ sitting up at the front of the pub next to the stage area. Beth walked straight into the toilets to fix up her hair and re-apply her lipstick. She came out and went straight to the bar to order a half pint of lager and lime. She sat down at the table nearest to the stage and waited.

Jenny and Emily soon arrived, and Beth greeted them with a smile. 'What took you so long,' she said.

Jenny sighed and replied, 'We missed the bloody bus.' 'How come you're here early then?'

'My dad gave me a lift,' said Beth as she lit a cigarette. It was Friday night and the girls were planning on a late one. They would usually stay at the pub until around eleven, then find a way of getting into town and spend the next four or five hours at the rock club in Manchester.

Beth kept an eager look at the door as she was praying that her bass player would turn up. 'He might not come here, Beth,' said Jenny.

'I know,' replied Beth. 'Still, there is no harm in looking.' The girls ordered drinks, and they made themselves comfortable for the night. Before long a trail of young men was surrounding the table with Beth laughing and all the girls flirting in fun. The pub started to get full with young teenagers entering in small groups and bikers stripping of their leather jackets and stacking their helmets on the bar. The music got louder and so did the voices, and the air became a thick haze of smoke. Beth ordered the drinks, and as she waited at the bar, she turned around and spotted her bass player who was just walking in through the door followed by the rest of the band members. *Oh my God*, she thought. *He is actually here. Just look casual now; don't let him see you all nervous.* Beth turned around to the girls and caught Jenny's eye. She couldn't hide her excitement, and Jenny knew who had just arrived. Back at the table, the girls exploded into laughter and giggles.

Beth ran to the toilet to double check her hair. When she returned she spotted the bass player stood at the bar. *Wow!* she thought. He was so tall, and his hair was truly beautiful, all shiny and pitch black, reaching right down to the tip of his bottom. He had the deepest brown eyes, and his smile made Beth melt instantly. Of course, he was surrounded by girls who were swooning for his attention. Beth's smile dissolved, and she shrank back in her chair. *I will never be able to have the courage to even talk to this guy, I am so stupid,* she thought. Jenny tried to distract her by introducing her to one of the bikers who had just come over to the table. 'Beth, this is Pete, and he has just offered to take one of us to the club tonight,' she said.

Pete was very good looking with olive skin and a black beard and moustache. His hair was shoulder-length, and he wore a red and white bandanna around his forehead. Beth glared at his muscular arms and couldn't resist shouting out, 'Oh, Pete, can you take me?' Pete just smiled, and Jenny sat down rather annoyed at Beth for jumping in on this one.

Pete asked Beth if she would like a drink and as soon as he had gone over to the bar, Jenny turned to Beth and said, 'Well, thanks, Beth, I really like him.'

'How was I supposed to know that and why did you introduce me to him in the first place if you wanted him to take you on his bike to the club?' replied Beth.

'I was just trying to distract you from the bar and the girls surrounding Jake, that's all,' Jenny said.

Beth felt totally guilty and apologised, 'Sorry, Jenny,'

'It's okay. I will ask someone else for a ride and Pete can take you, okay?' Jenny smiled back.

Meanwhile, Emily had snagged a tall guy who was leering all over her, which Emily loved. Beth turned around to spy on Jake who was talking to some tall blonde headed girl and Beth felt her disappointment rise. Pete headed back to the table, and Beth stood up and grabbed his arm. 'It's okay, Pete, I think I have got myself another ride, but thanks for offering,' she said. 'Jenny is looking for a ride though.' With that said, Beth made her way to the toilet. On the way back Led Zeppelin was playing, and a small group of people had got up "head banging" so Beth joined in. She felt incredibly sexy and free whilst she was dancing to the rhythm of the rock music and stayed up on the dance floor for a few more songs. When she returned to the table sweat was pouring down her face and made her curls spring tighter around her face which was flushed red. Beth took a big gulp of her lager. The girls partied on until it was time to leave the pub, Emily and Jenny both had found rides which left Beth hovering around at the entrance.

The next thing she knew, Jake was brushing past her, and he turned to smile. 'Looking for a ride to the club?' asked Jake.

Beth could not believe he was speaking to her. 'Yes, I am, do you have a ride?' she said.

'No,' replied Jake, 'but there's room in the van for one more if you like?'

Beth didn't need asking twice and followed Jake over to a white van parked across the road. 'I'm Jake, what's your name?' Beth stuttered before saying her name, and the two of them climbed into the back seat of the van.

When the other band members had climbed in Jake introduced them to Beth. 'Hello, Beth,' they replied. Beth was in her element, and Jake talked to her all the way to Manchester.

8

Ava walked energetically towards the bus stop to make her way to Ashton Town Centre where she would meet Angela. They were both off to catch a movie at the local cinema on Market Street. The girls met every Sunday and had been doing so for a few years, unbeknown to Brian, who automatically thought his obedient wife was safely sat on a pew over at the local church. Ava knew he hated anything to do with church and this gave her a well-needed advantage, one which helped her gain some small amount of personal freedom, which Ava so desperately lived for each week. She did not dare think of the consequences if Brian should ever find out that she had been lying to him. Ava was so unhappy with her life that the thought of being caught out by her manipulating fuck of a husband somehow seemed pushed to the back of her mind. She was free and intended to enjoy the experience; even the deceit a little!

Angela was standing with a small crowd of people when Ava's bus entered the bus station. She was a well-built woman, several years younger than her friend, and her hair was bleached blonde flowing down her back. Angela was not afraid of make-up with her bright blue eye shadow and red lips sealing a mouthful of yellow teeth. She wore a pair of blue jeans which were tucked into a pair of brown leather boots. There were fragments of a polka dot blouse sticking out from beneath Angela's navy blue padded coat. Ava waved and smiled as soon as she saw her partner in crime. 'Hello there stranger, long time no see,' smiled Angela with a fag hanging out of her mouth. 'Come on we're going to miss the first bit of the film.' Ava almost had to run to keep up with her mate as they bustled through the crowd waiting to board the bus and crossed over into the shopping mall. They passed the large fish and chip shop before crossing Old Road, where the old, worn down Odeon

Cinema was positioned on the corner. They climbed the mound of steps leading to the cinema's entrance.

Inside Ava and Angela bought a selection of sweets and fizzy drinks and made their way to their seats, just as the lights dimmed and the previews began. 'Just in time hey, Ava,' Angela said with a mouthful of chocolate. Ava just smiled with her eyes on the large screen. The renowned movie *The Empire Strikes Back* started around fifteen minutes later and both the girls thoroughly enjoyed the film, along with nine hundred other patrons making the small cinema almost full.

Two hours later, Ava and Angela left the old building and stopped at the fish and chips shop across the road from the Odeon and sat down inside to devour a plate full of chips and gravy, which was washed down with two cups of hot tea. 'So, sweetheart, how's your weekend been?' asked Angela.

'You know the answer to that one,' Ava said. 'My life is just heaven, Angela, and I couldn't be happier.'

'Well, at least you have a husband, not like mine who went and died on me,' replied Angela. 'Look I know you are hiding a lot, and I can't think why you can't talk to me about it, Ava.'

Ava hesitated and burst into tears. 'Are you all right, Av?' asked Angela.

Ava just hung her head low and sobbed. 'I'm so sorry. I didn't mean to cry, I just can't keep doing this,' replied Ava.

Angela grabbed hold of her hand and whispered, 'Let's get out of here, too many prying eyes.' They left swiftly and walked towards Stamford Street to blend into the crowd of shoppers. They found a quiet spot between the large buildings and sat down on a wooden bench.

Ava looked at Angela and said, 'I have to leave him, and you have to help me.'

'Of course, honey, I will help you all I can, you know that, but just tell me what the hell is going on?' replied Angela.

'He is a monster, Ang,' said Ava. 'He keeps me locked up in that prison, and I can't do it anymore, I just can't.'

'My husband is all show, and to everyone else, he is the nicest, politest person you would ever want to meet, but with me he is cruel, and I feel invisible with no presence what so ever. We sleep in separate beds and have done so for over twenty years. I have to wash his clothes and make his fucking meals; I

46

feel like his fucking mother, not his wife. I hate having sex with him as it is so cold and harsh. He never treats me as an equal, he just orders me around, and I just can't stand it any longer.'

'Okay, sweetheart, we need to make a plan on how we are going to get you away from that scumbag,' replied Angela.

'It's hopeless, Ang, where would I go? And he would only find me and drag me back.'

'Do you have any savings, Ava?' asked Angela.

'Not much as Brian controls everything, even my wages, I have to give the pay packet straight to him on Thursday nights, when I get paid.'

'Christ, Ava, do you get any of the money for yourself?' said Angela.

'He gives me fifty pounds, and he buys all the groceries and pays all the bills. The rest he puts away for our savings. I have managed to put a little away, Ang, I think I have about three hundred pounds tucked away in my underwear drawer.'

'You're going to need more than that, Ava, if you really are serious about leaving him,' replied Angela. 'We had better get you back as he will be wondering where you are, and we don't want to cause any suspicions, not now,' Angela said as she pulled Ava up off the bench. They raced back to the bus station and hopped on a bus which was ready to pull away from the station. 'Don't worry, Ava, I will help you all I can,' promised Angela. 'We can talk about it more tomorrow at work.'

Ava just nodded her head gently and smiled. She stood up from her seat as her bus stop came into view, 'See you at work tomorrow,' Angela said as Ava stepped off the bus. She walked back to Cedar Lane, and as she opened her front door a familiar aroma hit both her nostrils, it was the smell of burning pork.

9

Beth raced down the long driveway to her house and frantically grabbled with her keys to open the front door. Inside Tina ran down the stairs to prance around and adorn Beth with licks and grunts. 'Hello, my baby girl,' Beth shouted lifting Tina up into her arms. Beth cuddled Tina whilst she nestled her head into Beth's warm body. 'Have you missed me, baby? Well, I'm home now.' Beth put Tina down and climbed the stairs, quickly stopping off at her bedroom where she threw down her bag. 'Come on, girl let's go for your walk,' Beth said grabbing Tina's lead. The pair walked down the street, and Beth lit up a cigarette while Tina sniffed the ground and found a comfortable spot to pee on. 'Have to make this a short walk girl, as I have to keep my eye on the time.' They headed back towards Birch Lane, and both raced into the house. It wasn't long before both of them were snuggled up on the sofa. Beth's father arrived home soon after and woke Beth up to ask if she wanted to go with him to pick up Jane. 'Sorry, Dad, I can't as I have to have a shower and get ready for going out. *Fire* is playing live at the pub tonight, and I can't be late as I want to get front row seats.'
James smiled and headed for the stairs. 'See you when we get back luv,' he said as the front door closed with a bang. Beth went quickly back to sleep.

She woke up startled and jumped up causing Tina to fall off the edge of the sofa where she was snoozing alongside her mistress. 'Sorry, girl, did I frighten you,' said Beth half asleep. She noticed that her parents had returned and were both in bed taking a nap. Beth quickly telephoned Jenny to make sure all was still on for their night out. 'Hi, it's me,' said Beth. 'What time you meeting me?'

Jenny replied, 'I have to wait for my sister to get back before I can leave so I will have to meet you at the pub.'

'Okay,' said Beth. 'You know we have to get there early, don't you, to save the best seats.'

'Yes, you go ahead and I'll meet you there,' said Jenny.

'Okay, see you when you get there, I will be leaving here around 6.30 pm,' said Beth with a worried look on her face. The girls said their goodbyes and hung up.

Beth ran towards the shower and quickly washed her hair and dried herself. She pulled on her favourite blue jeans and knee-length black leather boots her dad had bought her last winter when she was recovering from the flu. She chose her Pink Floyd T-shirt from the Wall Tour and grabbed her red leather bikers' jacket. Beth popped her head into her parents' bedroom and shouted, 'See you two later, I'm off to the pub.'

'Okay, luv, be careful,' replied her mother.

Beth placed her cigarettes, lighter and chewing gum into her black leather saddle bag, along with her purse and picked up Tina for a last minute squeeze. 'You be good now girl, and I'll see you later.' Beth headed down the stairs and quickly marched up the driveway to the bus stop. The night air was turning chilly and there was still enough daylight around. Beth's hair was still wet, and she shivered slightly waiting for the bus to come. *I hope you come soon, bus; I really do need to get to the pub and snare my seats.* Beth was infatuated with the bass player, and tonight she was going to try and pluck up enough courage to speak to him.

As she was waiting for the bus, a navy blue car drove past and pulled up about 50 yards further up the road. Beth heard the car horn and turned to see if she could recognise the driver. She then started walking towards the car, hoping it was someone she knew who would give her a lift as the bus seemed to be taking ages and she would be pissed if it made her late, tonight of all nights. Beth reached the blue Ford Cortina, and the passenger window was rolled down.

Inside Beth saw a man who she definitely didn't know; he had a bald head, was in his mid to late forties and wore thick black glasses. The man smiled gently at Beth and said Hello. 'Thought you might need a lift, where you off tonight?' said the stranger.

Beth looked more closely in the car, it seemed pretty new and was immaculate. She stared into the man's eyes and listened to his tone of voice. 'I'm going to Stalybridge to the *Dog and Hound* pub,' replied Beth.

'Oh, I am going that way, I can drop you off if you like,' said the man.

Beth thought about waiting for the bus that might never come and the thought of arriving too late at the pub to get her important seat was nagging at her. 'Okay, that's great,' Beth said as she opened the passenger side door and climbed into the car. As soon as the door closed and the car was in motion, Beth felt a terrible ache from the pit of her stomach which rose immediately to her throat. *Oh my God, what have I done?* she thought. But it was too late.

Two minutes into the drive and Brian found himself glowing on the inside. He had spent many cold nights and days pursuing this young maiden, and it had finally paid off. He knew she would be hard to get into the car but didn't count on it being that easy. Meanwhile, Beth was trying to compose herself, and she had watched a TV program once on killers where the victim had escaped because she told the killer all about herself and this led him to see that she was a real human being. Beth quickly started chatting, 'My name is Beth and I'm 18 years old, I live with my mum and dad just where you picked me up. I have a cute little poodle called Tina and I am studying Art at Beaufort Road College. I want to be a famous artist one day.' Brian said nothing, just smiled and nodded in agreement. The more Brian sat in silence, the more Beth became nervous, and she noticed that for the minute, the stranger was driving in the right direction towards Stalybridge.

As they passed by the Town Centre Beth grew even more anxious, she blurted out, 'You can let me out here please, mister.' Brian knew that this was the time when his passengers usually got agitated, which could become dangerous when they started thrashing about in the front seat of his car. He turned towards Beth and punched her hard in the side of her face. Beth's body went limp, and Brian turned on his cassette player and resumed driving. He drove through Stalybridge onto Huddersfield Road and headed for Upper Mill which was a quiet country place where he could stop off without causing too much attention. He soon reached a small village named Saddleworth and came upon an isolated spot in the road where there were trees on either side.

He turned his main lights off and checked around to make sure there was no traffic behind him or approaching on the road in front. He smoothly rolled the car off the road and headed for the lush, overgrown fence line of trees. When safely hidden in the foliage Brian turned off the engine.

Beth awoke and felt cold; she was lying on her side on a blanket of some sort and noticed she was naked, yet covered with a sleeping bag. There were dim lights around her on the ground, they looked like candles. She tried to move her arms, which were behind her, but they were tied tightly with some kind of rope. Beth looked up and saw the car she had been abducted in and heard music coming from inside the vehicle. *Oh God, where is he? Please God, help me, I don't want to die.* Beth tried frantically to loosen the rope around her wrists but it was futile, they were just too tight. Brian emerged from the back of the car carrying a basket and sat down beside Beth on the woollen rug he had carefully laid out on the cold grass. 'My lovely, you're awake,' he said. 'I hope you are not too cold, my dear? I have some tasty treats for us and the wine will help to warm you.' He placed his hand into the basket and pulled out a bottle of wine and two glasses, followed by a plastic tub filled with strawberries and other various appetizers. Beth tried to keep calm by telling herself: just do what he tells you to and you may get out of this alive. Beth was not going to give up without a fight. She tried to speak, but her throat was dry and she couldn't stop shaking. Eventually, the words came, and she asked the man if he could untie her hands. Brian smiled and replied, 'Not yet my beauty.' He poured the wine and put a glass to Beth's lips where she drank eagerly. Do whatever he wants became her mantra.

Brian then offered her a strawberry holding it delicately in his hand and feeding her with delight. He then started to undress, and Beth prepared herself for what was to come. He lay beside her underneath the cover with his cold, clumsy hands mauling her body. 'Oh, pretty one how soft you feel and so warm,' Brian sneered. Beth tried to think of something else and pretended she was home in her bed and this was just a terrible nightmare which she would soon wake from. She could feel his foul breath on her face as he started to kiss her cheek and work his way around to her lips. Beth felt she would throw up, but held back as she wanted him to think she was enjoying herself. Brian lay on his back and pulled Beth up onto his chest and positioned her on his penis which sank inside her. Beth screamed inside as he began moving her up and down writhing in his sick pleasure. *Please God, let me be okay, I don't want to die.* The act continued with Brian moaning and groaning and Beth biting her bottom lip so hard so as to stop her from screaming out loud. When he had climaxed, he pushed Beth off him, and she rolled back on her side onto the blanket.

He lay there for a while in silence and then started to speak. 'You are the chosen one, my sweet, and I am your master. You will now perform the dance of death and offer yourself to the Earth God.' He seemed to be in a trance-like state and almost delirious as he pulled Beth up to her feet.

Beth started to think sharply and said, 'Yes, Master, I will do whatever you command, but please untie these ropes so I can dance more freely for you.' She looked into his glazed dark eyes and said, 'Can I please you more before the dance?' Brian grinned and pulled her down to her knees. He thrust his penis into her hands and started motioning them up and down his erected organ. Beth nearly vomited but did what he motioned her to do. 'Is this to your liking, Master?' Beth knew this was keeping her alive for longer, long enough for her to think of how she could escape this maniac.

When he had had his fill, Brian stood upright and walked towards the boot of his car. As he approached her, Beth could see something shimmering in his right hand. *Oh my God, it's a fucking knife, he's going to kill me. Oh God, no, please.*

Brian turned the volume up on his car stereo and the *Rite of Spring* played part II much to Brian's enchantment and Beth's horror. 'Dance my chosen one. Dance for all your worth,' he bellowed.

Beth began to move and twirl around with tears streaming down her face, and she felt sick and frightened. 'Please don't kill me,' she pleaded as the killer just laughed and demanded she dance faster and faster. Beth tried to remain strong as thoughts of her parents, family and little Tina flashed through her head. She wanted to be at home safe, and now she knew that she may never see them again. She had to get away from this psycho, and she had to think fast. Beth became dizzy and fell to the ground and, before she could orientate herself, Brian had pulled her to her feet. She vomited, and he pushed her away so as to keep from getting sprayed with bile. 'Please, I don't know what you want, but please I will do anything, please let me live,' Beth begged.

'Oh, my loveliness, that I cannot do, you must be sacrificed, for it is written in the stars, it is your fate,' Brian decreed. He began to approach Beth for a second time and this time she tried to run with all her strength. She began heading into the thick mass of trees. 'It's no use, my dear, you can't get far,' Brian yelled as he went back to his boot and pulled out a large torch. He shone the light on the darkness and followed Beth into the wooded area.

Beth ran hysterically in the blackness and could feel sharp twigs and rocks rip into the bare soles of her feet, but she kept on running. Scared and all alone, Beth uttered to herself over and over again, *Just keep running, come on, you can do this.* Brian was not far away and could see her up ahead in the near distance. He could not run, as he was out of condition and he knew it. She would tire soon and fall then he would catch her and drag her back to the car and make the sacrifice. Brian's heart rate was raised, and he found he was again aroused with his penis erect. He was still naked, however; he felt nothing but pure adrenaline running through his veins.

Beth had no idea where she was running to; it was so dark, and she could not see any lights or recognisable signs or houses. She ran and ran with the light from Brian's torch in the distance, and she knew that if she stopped, he would kill her. She could feel her heart racing as she struggled with the enormous fear rising in every part of her being. *Oh God, please let me live.* Beth didn't see the large drop around four feet at the edge of the trees, and she fell heavily into the dried up creek below. As she hit the surface, she heard a crack and felt a tremendous shooting pain run up her left leg. She quickly tried to stand, and her leg gave way with excruciating agony. Beth hid in the side of the banking and heard the sounds of her killer approach. She held her breath and pressed deep into the side of the grassy bank. Brian knew she had come this way and slid down the deep grassy verge. Beth had no chance of running from him as he grabbed her hair and dragged Beth to the floor. She screamed in pain and became unconscious.

When Beth came to consciousness, she was back at the car and lay on the blanket where all this nightmare had begun. *Why on Earth did I get into that car? What a fool I have been.* She saw Brian approach and could see clearly the large, glimmering knife in his hand. He knelt down beside her and plunged the cold steel into her chest with all his strength. Beth felt no pain as she lay there in the cold night air. She looked into those black eyes of evil, and the world went dark.

10

Harry stood in his small, modern kitchen, buttering his toast when the phone rang. He leant over the bench and picked up the receiver and spoke. 'Hi, Harry here.'

'Hello, Harry, it's George Wilson, you better get down here; we have another one.' George was the leading detective at Hyde Police station investigating a recent case of three local girls who had gone missing over the past 12 months.

'Okay, George, I'm on my way,' said Harry putting down the phone. He had been working with the local cops for a few years now on missing persons and the odd murder investigation. Earlier in the year, the police were not sure if the girls were victims of the notorious Yorkshire Ripper, but he had just confessed to a series of brutal killings with no mention of these young teenage girls. The case looked like being a completely different murder case, and Harry's help was invaluable.

Harry's psychic abilities included clairsentience or a form of extra-sensory abilities which allow him to acquire certain knowledge just by feeling or touching items belonging to the person/s that have gone missing. Harry can also gain important information just by being at a crime scene or when tracing the last known steps of victims. His mediumship skills had always played a separate role in Harry's life where he travelled around to various spiritualist churches in the country and contacted the dead for grieving family members.

Harry poured dry biscuits in Ollie's food bowl and checked he had clean water, then grabbed his car keys and closed the door. Fifteen minutes later he was parking his Mini outside Hyde Police station. He entered the blue doors at the front of the red brick building and made his way to the main reception desk. Harry was handed a security card with his photograph on it and was escorted into the main part of the building. He passed several interview rooms and found himself in a large workstation where uniformed police were sat at their desks. Beyond the desks were several rows of empty chairs facing a large wall full of photographs and information. Harry stepped up to the wall and noticed a new photograph of a young girl and underneath was her name neatly printed; Elizabeth Cotten, aged 18 years, missing from home for the past two days. Harry turned quickly as he felt a hand on his right shoulder, 'Thanks for coming, Harry,' said George, who was slightly taller than Harry and overweight.

George joined the police force when he was a young man, and he had worked his way up the chain of command. Police work ran in his family with his father and grandfather both completing successful careers in the force. George, like many police officers, worked long excruciating hours, often staying back at the station and missing out on family life. This came at a great cost for George, with his wife divorcing him a few years ago. He met his wife, Anna, at a local dance hall, when they were both just 18 years old, and they married two years later. The girls came along soon afterwards. George fell instantly in love with Anna, and she felt the same. Anna's parents loved George and accepted the fact that his job kept him away from home at times. Anna managed to tolerate George's job, but after thirty years of being a police widow, which is what the wives of police officers affectionately called it, she became tired. The girls had both left home, and Anna was fed up of spending long nights by herself in front of the TV. George had promised many times that he would cut down on his work, but there was always another crime to solve, and Anna gave up in the end. Anna worked at the local hospital as an administration officer, and she was often home alone with the two young girls while George was working frantically on a new case. They managed to buy a small semi-detached house in Ashton, which Anna renovated.

There was no other man involved, and the separation was very amicable. George gave Anna the home as he said he did not want to live in it without her. His two daughters are now adults with children of their own, which George rarely gets to see. He lives in a small bed unit now located in Hyde, not far from the police station and he really has nothing outside of his job. Since the divorce George pushed himself further into his work, often neglecting his health and eating take away and drinking far too much whiskey. His weight began to increase and with it, health problems associated with diabetes and heart complaints. In the earlier days, he would keep himself fit by going to the gymnasium and jogging each day. On the days he could get away from the station George would spend it with his two girls, fishing or taking trips away to the seaside. He used to take pride in his appearance, but now he was an overweight man who struggled to even shave in the mornings. He was one of the best detectives in the metropolitan area, and everyone knew his name. If George Wilson could not get a lead on a case, no one could. He wasn't a happy man by all accounts, but he did love his job. George never really got over Anna leaving him. He still loved her with all his heart, but he knew she was right, he was married to the job and how could he expect Anna to just sit in every night and have no life. He thought about his own parents and how his mother was often alone. He remembered all the arguments with mum yelling, 'You're never here.' It brought painful emotions back to George and how he missed his dad too, and how he would wait eagerly for his dad to come home from work, which he never did. In a way, George had also given up on life just like his wife had on their marriage and his mother before that.

George was in his mid-fifties, with silver-cropped hair and rough skin. He was wearing a crumpled old jacket and black trousers and wore a pale blue shirt with no tie. 'That's the new girl?' Harry asked pointing to the new photograph on the wall.

'Yeah, I'm afraid so, her parents phoned it in over the weekend when the kid didn't come home on Saturday morning. We are interviewing the parents today and would like you to come along and take a look at the girl's room if that's okay with you, Harry?' Detective Constable Mason said as he approached the two men. John Mason was a lot younger than his superior George. He had a good head of brown hair which needed cutting, and he wore brown trousers and a white shirt with a large coloured tie that was loosely wrapped around his collar.

'Yeah, that will be fine,' said Harry. He turned his gaze back to the girls' photos on the wall.

Eighteen-year-old Sandra Ellis was the first girl noted to have gone missing. She was last seen leaving her workplace, which was an old people's nursing home on Dewsnap Lane in

Dukinfield on the 23rd February, around 5 pm. She never arrived home, and her parents reported her missing that night. Harry had visited the house and checked out some of her personal belongings, but he couldn't get anything to help the police. Her photograph showed a pretty young face with fiery red shoulder-length hair wrapped around it and her big brown eyes. Her skin was fair and freckled, and she wore braces on her teeth.

The second photograph was of 19-year-old Emily Stevens, who was reported missing in April 1981, just five months ago, and she disappeared without a trace that evening on her way to a friend's birthday party. Emily was last seen walking down Mottram Road in Stalybridge at around 7 pm. Emily had naturally blonde curly hair to her shoulders, and she had the bluest eyes Harry had ever seen. She wasn't as pretty as Sandra, but her eyes were something else. Harry took one of Emily's bracelets and used his psychic abilities where he did seem to pick up some visions involving a blue car and a brown leather briefcase. The police traced all the blue cars in the local vicinity, but nothing came of it.

The third image on the wall was of Amanda Kirk who went missing in June, only a couple of months ago. She was older than the others by five or so years, and she had straight, short auburn hair with dark olive skin and dark eyes. She was last seen in Ashton and never turned up at the local pub that night where she was meeting her boyfriend. Harry had walked down the same street that Amanda was supposed to have taken called Penny Meadow in Ashton-Under-Lyne. He did feel a strange sense of surprise and saw images flash in his mind of loud music playing; some kind of classical music and he saw the blue car again, but that was not enough to assist the police. Harry looked at the new photograph of Elizabeth Cotten; she was extraordinarily beautiful and had the most welcoming smile, the kind that you would never forget. She had lots of curly dark brown hair and smooth ivory skin. It made Harry sick in the stomach looking at these young girls knowing that some psycho may, or probably had, murdered them.

The police car drove slowly and respectfully up the Cotten's driveway and parked outside the large semi-detached building. Harry rang the doorbell and was accompanied by George and John. Beth's father opened the door and greeted the men, where

George introduced his colleagues. James led them up the stairs, the same stairs Beth had raced up and down so many times in the past and directed them through to the living room. Jane came out of her bedroom with red eyes and tissues held up to her nose. 'Mrs Cotten, we are so very sorry to have to visit you on such a stressful occasion,' said George.

'That's okay,' replied Jane. 'Please take a seat and can I offer you a cup of tea?

'That's very kind of you, Mrs Cotten,' George said, 'but we are fine, thank you.'

George quickly introduced Harry and politely asked if Harry was allowed to view Beth's room. Jane nodded and James led Harry along the hallway to her bedroom. Harry stepped inside and immediately noted the ragged canvas bag at the foot of the door exactly where Beth had dropped it on Friday night. He smiled, picked it up, went over to her bed and sat down. As he was opening the bag to find a personal belonging of Beth's a small furry animal jumped up on the bed beside him. 'Well, hello there,' Harry said as he patted the dog. Tina just licked his hand and whimpered. 'I know you miss her,' said Harry. 'Let's hope she is okay and you get her back soon.' Harry reached further into the bag and pulled out a Sony Walkman. He put the earphones in his ears, pressed play and was suddenly rocking to the sounds of AC/DC. *This girl has really great taste in music,* he thought.

Harry switched the music off and continued to delve into the bag where he felt around until he came upon a small stone which was cold to touch. He pulled out his hand to examine the object more closely and recognised it immediately as it was a crystal of pink rose quartz. Harry sat on the bed and closed his eyes clutching the pink rock in his right hand. He suddenly felt an intense pain down his right leg and then a more shuddering pain in his chest. His breathing became shallow, and he nearly lost consciousness, but then he could hear a strange noise. It sounded like a voice talking at great speed, and Harry was unable to make sense of it. He sat up and noticed Beth's artwork decorating her small but warm and inviting room. *What a cool room and a talented artist in the making. Now come on, Beth, give me some help here.*

Harry moved over to her white wooden wardrobe and opened one of the doors where he saw voluminous clothes hanging clumsily from wooden hangers. He peered down at the bottom of the closet and saw an array of boots and shoes. Harry was a bit of a shoe freak himself and found himself picking up several pairs of Beth's sneakers admiringly. Harry's eyes flicked around the room once more before he closed the door respectfully and went back to the living room where he could hear George asking Beth's parents the awkward questions. 'Has your daughter ever run away from home? Does she have a boyfriend? Was she on drugs?' Harry had heard it all before and saw the same shocked reactions from the parents.

'Our Beth is a good kid, and she would never run away from us. She is very happy-go-lucky and determined to get into art school,' said Jane almost sobbing when she spoke.

'Mrs Cotten, please forgive me,' said George, 'I do not doubt that your daughter is what you say she is; but this is just routine, I do hope you understand.'

'Why aren't you out there looking for her?' scolded James and put his arm around his waning wife's shoulders as Jane sank into his chest sobbing.

'I just want my little girl back,' Jane cried.

The interview was terminated at this point with Jane too distraught to get anything useful out of her or from James, for that matter. The men made their exit quickly and swiftly stating they would be in touch and keep the Cottens up to date on any developments. 'Fuck, I hate that part of the job,' George said as he was driving out of the driveway with Harry and John nodding their heads. They drove past the same bus stop Beth had been waiting for her bus only a few days ago. Harry sensed a feeling of terror as he stared out of the back seat window watching the Cottens' residence slip away from view.

Back at the station George called for a meeting to go over strategies and receive important feedback from the police on the ground, who had been doing all the leg work. Hopefully, they would have come up with something. 'Okay,' said George standing at the front of the now filled rows of chairs in the large room at the rear of the station. George began to address the audience made up of uniformed police with their notebooks out and looking attentive. 'There has been another missing person added to our gallery, she is an 18-year-old female who was reported missing on Saturday morning by her parents when she did not arrive home from a night out with her friends. The girl's name is Elizabeth Cotten who was last seen by her parents at her home, before crossing Birch Lane on Friday night around 6.30 pm heading towards the bus stop. She was to arrive at the *Dog and Hounds* in Stalybridge Town Centre around 7 pm, but she never got there. Doug, what can you add to this?'

Doug cleared his throat and said, 'I have spoken to a number of Beth's close friends who were to meet her at the pub at 7 pm, Sir. They said she was really excited about being there to see this rock band and nothing would have kept her from going,' Doug paused and then continued, 'Her friends said that at 7.30 pm they knew she was not coming and that she must have been too sick or something. One of Elizabeth's closet friends named Jenny Colt said she went to the closest pay phone to call Elizabeth's home, Jenny said the phone rang out and no one picked it up. After several attempts, she went back to the pub to join her friends and although they were worried, they did not know what else to do. They stayed at the pub until closing time and headed off home instead of going into Manchester like they usually did.'

'Okay thanks, Doug, good work,' replied George.

'Do we have any other information? What about anyone who may have seen Elizabeth walking across Birch Lane? Or anyone who may have seen her get on the bus to Stalybridge?'

A young police officer stood up and replied, 'I did a door to door investigation, Sir, around Birch Lane and the local streets in that vicinity, but I got no eyewitnesses. Nobody saw a thing, Sir.'

'Thanks for that, Ian,' said George as he lit up another cigarette. 'Christ we have nothing and a possible four fucking murders here,' he raged. 'Someone somewhere must have seen something. Get back out there and start asking all over again,' he ordered.

John stood up and invited Harry to stand and address the men. 'Sorry guys I really don't have much to add at this point,' said Harry looking down at his blue sneakers. 'I did get some flashes of the blue car again while I was at Elizabeth's home, and I am going to look at some car brochures to try and narrow it down a bit more; to see if I can get a make or model, or something,' Harry sighed.

'I want some of you to go and interview the girl's friends again and find out everything you can about her habits, thoughts, what kind of person she is. See if she has any crushes on anybody? Did she keep a diary?' George shouted. 'Also, do some digging on all these girls and see if they knew each other? There has to be some connection here, we're just not seeing it.' George added. 'I want to meet up again in eight hours, and I want something good from you, get it?' George ordered.

The small group of uniformed men replied, 'Yes, Sir,' as they departed from the chairs and stirred into motion gathering their jackets and hats before vacating the station.

George looked at John and motioned him to his office. When inside George put his hand to his forehead and said, 'Fuck, John, we've got piss all on this, and the fucker is turning into a serial murder investigation, I can feel it in my bones. If I am right, the press won't be too far behind us, and then there is the boss, who will fucking kill me if we don't get a move on with this shit.'

John lit a cigarette and held his head down. 'We don't know if it is a serial killer, George, they might have just gone missing, right?'

'Well, my money is on the fucker being out there killing these young girls, and the fucker is smart,' George replied.

'We don't have a fucking scrap of evidence and no fucking bodies,' John replied.

Meanwhile, Harry worked with another police officer who showed him pictures of different makes of cars. Harry's face was full of resolve as he trolled through picture after picture of cars, trying to get a clear picture in his mind of the blue car, which had begun to haunt him. It was no use, Harry could not see anything clearly.

11

Beth opened her eyes to a dim orange light that was softly acquainting her sight to the strange surroundings. She was lying down with her head slightly propped up and felt closed in. Above her feet which were poking out of some kind of blanket, Beth could see a window. She tried to raise her head to be able to see clearly, but she was unable to move. Beth's memory came flooding back and with it, the intense fear of what she had experienced. *Oh God, where am I? Please don't let me be kidnapped by that freak.* Beth remembered getting into his car and felt so ashamed of how stupid she had been. She tried to block out the visions of that beast raping her, but it was useless; she saw the man's cold dark eyes and felt him inside of her while all the time screaming internally with horror. *Why can't I move? He must have given me something to knock me out or paralyze me? Where the fuck am I? Oh, mamma, I need you, please come and find me.* Beth realised she was in the back seat of the man's car parked under a lamp on a desolate street somewhere. She had no idea of how long she had been there or what day or even what time it was. She knew from the street light that it was night time. Beth lay motionless for hours staring at the window and thinking of home and her warm bed. *Someone please find me.* She tried to shout, but no noise came from her dry and grainy throat. Beth suddenly felt tired and her eyes slowly closed.

The next time Beth was conscious she witnessed the sun creeping into the cloud-filled sky spreading its filtered light rays over the street and seeping slowly into the car where Beth lay trapped. *Thank God, it's daylight, someone is bound to see me now when they walk by.* She tried so hard to move this time using all her strength, but it was futile. Her body felt like a heavy lump of meat glued to the leather seat beneath her. Beth focused on the little bit of view she had from the window and waited.

At seven o'clock sharp; Brian grabbed his thick, brown, corduroy, knee-length coat and his old faithful briefcase and closed his front door. Monday mornings were always hectic at work and on the roads, so he liked to leave in plenty of time. Beth's eyes began focusing on someone walking over towards the car; she felt a surge of excitement as this may be her chance of escape. She tried to call out or make any sound that the person might hear and free her. It wasn't long before Beth realised it was not going to be that way as the person quickly approaching the car by now was the piece of scum Beth had no problems identifying. *Oh God, no, please no, he's coming back for me, please no.* Beth became panicked and found herself feeling lightheaded and nauseous. *What the fuck, what can I do now?* She had no time to decide as Brian opened the car door on the driver's side and slid awkwardly into his seat. He threw his coat and briefcase onto the passenger seat and closed the door with a bang. Beth closed her eyes and prayed he would think she was still out for the count. Brian didn't seem to notice her and lit a cigarette as he drove away from the street. He turned on his radio and wound the window down sticking his arm out and resting his elbow on the rim humming to the music. It was a good day for Brian, he felt enriched from his sacrificial business on Friday night. He headed towards Manchester on the A635 toward his office without a care in the world.

As he turned in to the car park Beth stirred feeling the slowing down of the engine. *Where is he taking me? I can't even move. I have no chance here, oh please, someone help me.* Brian switched off the engine, grabbed his belongings and motioned himself out of the seat and locked the door; without a glance into the back seat. He walked slowly towards the building where he would spend the rest of the day sifting through numbers and figures. He hated the job and found it deathly boring, however; it served a purpose, as it kept Brian in the kind of lifestyle he liked.

Beth opened her eyes and couldn't believe it! He had just completely ignored her. Well, she felt safe for the time being, but Beth knew he would be back. She tried to move again and was becoming extremely frustrated with her body. Beth closed her eyes once more and began to cry. 'Do not cry, child.' Beth's eyes widened as she found the sound coming from a tall man with a gentle face who was now sitting in the front passenger seat and now turned towards her.

'Who are you? And how did you get in here?' gasped Beth.

'My name is Michael, and I am here to help you,' he replied with a soothing voice and kind smile.

'How did you know I was in here? And how are you going to help me?' Beth said with a puzzled and defensive expression on her young face. She noticed that the man was wearing a grey suit with a white shirt and matching grey tie. His face was clean shaven, and his hair was neatly cut around his ears. His eyes were a beautiful silver grey. He had the kindest face Beth had ever seen, and his eyes were like pools of rich shimmering liquid. Beth found herself almost drawn to those eyes and she felt an overwhelming sense of calm when he spoke.

'My dear child, you have suffered a great ordeal. Do you remember what happened to you?' the man said. Beth was in complete shock, she had no idea what was happening and started to feel queasy in her stomach.

'I know I was attacked by the guy who will be coming back any minute,' she said trying to clear her throat. She was amazed that her voice had now somehow returned. 'Can you get me out of here? I want to go home.'

The man smiled and replied, 'Elizabeth, you do not need to worry about that man hurting you ever again, I am here to protect you.'

'Well, get me out of here then,' Beth replied with dire urgency written all over her face. 'I can't seem to move at all, do you think he drugged me?' she added.

'Elizabeth,' the man spoke again in a calm but firm voice, 'I want you to listen to me very carefully, and I want you to promise me that you will not feel afraid, can you promise me that?' Beth paused and then nodded. 'You were indeed attacked by that man on Friday evening, and I am so sorry to tell you this, my dear child, but you died in this car that very same night.'

Beth's mind was in overdrive as she had heard the words clearly coming from the man's mouth, yet she felt in another place far away. The words "you died" kept playing over and over again in her head. Beth could not comprehend. *Is this a nightmare I'm having? Am I really dead? Oh God, this can't be happening to me, I want to see my mum.* The man continued.

'You were in so much shock that night, and sometimes when a person is subjected to such horror, they remain behind in their earthly body. I am here today to guide you, Elizabeth, to the place where you should have transitioned to shortly after you took your last breath.'

Beth sighed and began to cry once more. 'I don't want to be dead, I want to go home,' she sobbed.

The man leant over and was able to hold Beth's hands in his. She felt a loving presence as he did this and began to feel lighter and more at ease. *Who was this guy?* she thought. 'What will happen to that monster that killed me?' Beth blurted out. 'He deserves to be dead, not me, it's not fair.'

Michael nodded his head and spoke once more. 'That is no longer your concern, my child, for your place on this Earth plane is done. Will you trust me and let me take you where you belong?'

Beth suddenly felt no fear or pain, and she noticed her body beginning to move somewhat. Soon she was sitting upright in the back seat of the car with full control of her limbs. She looked down and noticed she was wearing the same clothes she wore on Friday night, with no signs of any blood or damage. 'Michael,' she said hesitantly. 'What if I refuse to go with you now? What if I choose to stay and get that pig put behind bars?'

Michael looked deep into Beth's frightened eyes and smiled. 'You do have free will, my dear, although, I would not advise you to stay here, but I cannot force you to come away with me.'

Beth thought about her choices, she was tired and scared of being trapped in this vehicle, yet somewhere deep inside her she felt an unexplainable urge to stay and get justice for her life that had been so cruelly cut short. She thought some more before replying, 'I can't go with you, Michael, not yet.' Beth sighed and lowered her head.

'Then you must do what you think is right,' replied Michael. 'I will send someone to help you. You will not have long here before the choice will be gone, my dear,' Michael added. 'I will take my leave now and do not worry for we shall meet again soon.' Beth raised her eyes to meet his and he disappeared just as quickly as he had appeared. Beth was left in awe. She still could not believe what that man had said about her dying and that she had stayed behind. *Wow*, she thought, *is this really happening?*

12

Ava stood at the raised bench dispensing medication staring at the clock willing it to move faster so she could go on her lunch break with Angela. She had not been able to sleep since their weekly meet up where Ava had come clean about her sad life. She so desperately wanted to leave that pig but Ava could not see a way out. Two minutes to one, Ava grabbed her lunch from the fridge out back and made her way outside the shop around the corner to a small cornered off area filled with small tables and chairs. This is where the girls would catch up each day for lunch. Angela was late arriving, and Ava was already tucking into her ham and salad sandwich when Angela sat down beside her. 'Are you okay, sweetheart? Angela said.

'Yes, Angela, I am okay; I just don't know what I am going to do,' replied Ava in between a mouthful of food.

Angela was not the brightest tool in the shed, but she was a good listener and felt very close to Ava. The pair discussed Ava's plight and came up with a plan of getting Ava away safely. Angela instructed Ava to get her hands on as much money as she could over the next few weeks. It meant that Ava would have to come up with something that she would tell Brian she really needed. This was dangerous as Brian was very controlling on their expenses, however; if approached at the right time, he could be quite generous.

Angela had spoken to her sister who had a spare room in her house, which Ava could rent. Angela had also found a support centre in Hyde where Ava could go for advice, and she handed Ava the card with all the details on it. Ava slipped it carefully into her coat pocket, and the girls returned to the chemist. Ava decided to walk home from work that night as she needed the time to think. *Brian would be in his puny shed out the back anyhow; he only came in for his ritual dinner.* Ava thought about how her life had come to this. She was happy once, way back when she was at university. Her parents were both still alive then and she looked forward to going home in the summer break. Life was simple on the farm, but Ava loved her life back in Croatia. The days were long but filled with fresh air and sun beaming down on your back as you harvested the crops and fed the animals. She worked hard on the land to help out her parents, and Ava felt a sense of achievement in doing so.

Each night the family would retire around the large wooden table in the kitchen and eat the fruits of their labour laughing and talking of the day's events. Ava had never been so happy. *Oh, Momma and Papa, how I miss you both.* It had all begun to go horribly wrong the moment she met Brian. He was kind to her then and even her parents liked him, but he soon changed after they married. The separate sleeping arrangements followed, and Ava found herself lonelier than ever. Her contact with her parents was the only thing she had to look forward to, and when her mother became ill, Brian had forbidden her from going home to take care of her. Ava was allowed to go back for the funeral, and she often wondered why she ever returned to England. Her father died a few years later leaving Ava all alone in the world. *Nothing to go back to now anyhow*, she thought. The wind had begun to strengthen, and Ava wrapped her coat closer to her body. She felt the cool rush of air upon her face which reminded her she was still alive and breathing. She saw couples passing her in the twilight, some holding hands and smiling. Why had this seemed foreign to her? She had never been shown such affection from her husband. He was a cold, heartless pig, and Ava knew she had to leave him, but the trouble was, could she ever do it? She knew he had money, as Ava was left with a small inheritance after her farm was sold. *I need to get hold of some money and quickly.*

13

Beth didn't have to wait long before her help had arrived. Edward sat grinning on the back seat of the car alongside Beth with the pair just looking at each other. 'Hi, Beth, I'm Edward.' Beth smiled and looked at the odd young man sat beside her. He was wearing a white shirt and strange black trousers that were almost skin-tight, and he had these unusual black shoes which were pointed at the toe. His hair was fair and there were lots of it, sort of bunched up in a quiff on the top of his head.

Beth had a feeling this boy wasn't from the 1980s, and she was right. It turned out Michael had sent Beth her young uncle who had passed away in the 1960s when Beth had not even been born. Edward was 16 years of age when his life was cut short. He had been the youngest of eight siblings and the only son remaining at the family's home. Edward had just finished school and started working in a wood factory making brushes and other domestic appliances. His world had just begun; with a few pounds in his pocket each weekend Edward and his closest friend, his cousin Johnny, hit the town for some fun. Edward was known as the mischievous one who was always getting into some trouble or other. The girls swarmed around him like bees to honey. He was never without a pretty girl by his side. The day of the accident Edward had just been released from the hospital after cutting through most of his fingers on his right hand. That wasn't enough to stop Edward, as he mounted his girlfriend's large white male horse. He galloped down the lane to Mill Brook centre where his friends and Johnny hung out. He had just seen Beth's mum and waved to her from her front window. Someone let off a firecracker outside the small row of local shops, and the horse was freaked causing Edward to lose his grip on the reigns. Edward was thrown violently from the large beast and landed head first onto the concrete pavement. Edward died instantly.

Edward was the loving son of Sally and William Knightly. He was the youngest of seven siblings with his big sister, Margaret being the eldest, with over 30 years' difference in age. Sally had become pregnant unexpectedly at the age of 45 years. In between Margaret and Edward came two other sisters, one being Beth's mother, Jane and her aunty Rose. Then there were the three boys, William junior, John and Mark. William senior or "Billy" as he was referred to was the only son from his family and was rather spoilt. His father was also a policeman towering over six feet tall. He wore a large black cape over the top of his uniform and paraded a very unusual black moustache that curled up on the ends. He was always seen patrolling the streets with his big black truncheon ready to thrash anyone or anything that got in his way.

Billy's mother ran a fruit and vegetable shop which flourished in the small town of Carbrook. His parents bought another similar business for William and Sally as a wedding gift, however; Billy lacked the business skills of his mother and sisters. Sally tried her best to keep the shop open, but she had several young children to look after. Billy could be found at any of the local pubs where he would have a few pints of beer and then begin singing to the grateful audience that had usually congregated into the small smoky rooms of the establishment. Billy had the most wonderful voice and people could sit for hours listening to him, and they often did. Sometimes they would sing along with him, and Billy was in heaven. After a few more pints Billy would find himself involved in fights where he was often escorted to the police lockup to sober up. Poor Sally Knightly, she had only the support of her eldest daughter Margaret to try and keep the shop running smoothly. In the end, they lost their business, and despite Billy's parents providing another, the same outcome was inevitable. Sally found herself working full-time at the local cotton mill and Billy, well, he found work everywhere including driving coaches, manual labouring and truck driving. No matter what was said of Billy, he always found work and provided food on the table for his family.

At the time of the accident Beth's mother was married herself and had three young children. She lived a few houses down from her parents on Buckton Drive. The street was made up of large brick homes with two bedrooms and a small garden at the front and back. Carbrook was surrounded by rolling green hills and nearly every child growing up in that area had a horse or knew someone who was riding one. Edward spent a lot of time with his cousin John or *Johnny*. This was Margaret's only son, and they were born just a few months apart. Edward would always join the family for holidays; he was always at Johnny's house. The two boys were very close and inseparable. Margaret lived opposite her parents and Sister Jane, so it was easy for Edward and Johnny to pop in and out of the two houses. They were both really into music with Edward playing the guitar and Johnny learning to play the drums. Johnny's father had set up the drum kit in the spare room, and the young boys spent many a night jamming in there. Rock and roll music was all the rage, and the two teenagers idolised Roy Orbison, Johnny Cash and Buddy Holly.

'Hi, Edward, pleased to meet you,' said Beth.

'Do you know who I am?' Beth moved her head from side to side. Still finding all this hard to believe. 'I am your mother's little brother Ed, I died before you were born.' Edward replied.

'Oh my God, my mum told me about you and how you died falling off a horse. She said your mum never got over it, in fact, the whole family never really came to terms with it,' said Beth.

'Yes, it took me a long time too,' replied Edward as his smile faded. 'Look, I know how you are feeling right now, Beth; I've been there, so to speak. It is scary not knowing who or what to believe anymore.' Beth couldn't speak, she just nodded her head. 'I know this sounds crazy but things will be better for you, I promise,' said Edward as he slid over to join Beth on the back seat.

'I am not so sure about that,' said Beth.

'Do you know what has happened to you?' asked Edward. Beth nodded again and tried to say the words but they wouldn't come. 'It's okay, you don't have to tell me out loud, as long as you're aware that you have passed away, that's a start.'

'I can't believe that,' replied Beth who could feel her voice rising in volume and she felt a surge of anger take over. 'I don't want to be fucking dead, I want to go home and wake up from this insane nightmare,' she added.

Edward moved in closer and looked into Beth's terrified eyes. 'Hey listen, it's all right, you are safe with me and once you decide to come with us, all this will go away.'

Beth wasn't convinced. 'I want the bastard who did this to me caught,' Beth said.

Edward knew what had happened to Beth from Michael and he had been told that Beth was having trouble leaving the Earth plane. He had no idea it was because she wanted revenge on her killer. *Shit, this girl is tougher than I realised,* he thought. 'Beth, how do you plan on doing that? Have you thought this through properly? I don't want to put the mockers on your plan but you are now dead and nobody can see you, let alone hear you. How are you going to do this?' The conversation was stopped abruptly by Brian returning to his car.

'Oh God, I hate this creep,' said Beth. Edward just nodded as he felt a wave of dread flow over his entire body. Beth cowered as the weird looking man entered the vehicle throwing his briefcase on the passenger seat. 'Oh God, please don't let him hurt me,' Beth squealed lying further down on the back seat.

Edward could see how frightened she was. 'What did this man do to do you, Beth?'

'He raped me and knifed me in the chest, Edward, that bastard took my whole life away from me, I hate him and he's going to pay, I swear,' replied Beth who was now shaking with tears rolling down her cheeks.

'I am so sorry, Beth, I know what it's like to suddenly have your life taken from you, it's like someone has just extinguished your light, and you suddenly find yourself in darkness, feeling afraid and all alone.' Edward continued, 'I was younger than you Beth when I fell off my mate's horse and that's all I remember, then blackness all around me.'

Beth stopped crying and sat up, 'What happened to you next?' she asked inquisitively.

'Michael was there and he took hold of my hand and told me not to be afraid. I suddenly saw beautiful light and felt so much love, it was incredible. I am not supposed to tell you anymore just yet Beth, Edward said.

'I am sorry, Edward, here's me carrying on like a selfish brat only thinking of my life being cut short and not even thinking of how you must be feeling with being back here.'

'It's okay, Beth, I am here to help my family, and I'm glad to be able to help you.'

'Edward,' Beth suddenly replied.

'Yes, cuz,' replied Edward grinning in the process.

'Why didn't I see Michael straight away like you did?'

Edward thought about his answer for a few minutes and then said, 'You were in shock, Beth, and Michael had to wait until you were more settled.' Beth smiled and as Brian made his daily drive home, the two youngsters giggled in the back with Brian being none the wiser. After Brian had locked his car and disappeared into his bungalow, the two got down to business. 'How are we going to get this arsehole, Beth,' asked Edward.

'I don't know but we can't let him get away with it and who knows how many other girls he's killed in the same way,' replied Beth. 'We need help, that's one thing I do know,' said Beth. 'We need to get the police involved. Come on, Edward, let's make our way to the local cop shop.' Beth tried to open the car door but, of course, it was locked. She smiled and turned to Edward, 'Can you help me out here or what?' she teased.

In all the excitement of meeting his niece, Edward had forgotten why he was here. His orders were to assist Beth and that meant he had to show her a few tricks of the trade, so to speak, and more importantly, to warn her of the possible dangers she could encounter. 'Beth, we need to go over some basics first before I let you out of this car,' he began.

Beth turned to Edward inquisitively, 'Okay, Edward, you've got my attention now,' she smiled.

'Well, first there are some rules I need to explain to you, kiddo,' Edward grinned feeling all-important all of a sudden. 'The first one is the most important one, Beth, because it's about your safety while we are both still here. Because you um died in this car, well um,' Edward awkwardly continued, 'well this is what we call your base, if you like.'

'My what?' sniggered Beth.

'Come on, Beth, you have to take this seriously,' Edward said.

'Okay, I'm listening, really I am,' replied Beth.

'Right then,' Edward continued. 'You cannot leave your base for more than several hours because if you do, you won't be able to return to it. That would mean you would be shut out of your protective zone and you would have to walk among the dead in limbo.' Edward checked Beth's response as he knew this was pretty scary stuff for a newbie, well, that's what he liked to call people who had just left their earthly bodies. He saw Beth's smile slowly depart from her face and Edward hesitated as to whether to continue or not. Beth looked into his blue eyes and confirmed she was okay, so Edward felt it safe to move on. 'If you should see any other spirits when we are outside this car, you are to turn your face away from them, do I make myself clear?' He paused to check in with Beth.

'Sure I understand,' said Beth.

'Like Michael said we really do not have much time here before you must transition on, and if you refuse that time, then I'm afraid, Beth, you will be left here to walk alone with the other lost souls.' Beth shuddered and urged Edward to tell her more. 'One thing that you really need to understand, Beth, is that if you can't get back in here, you are not only in danger from the wanderers out there, but you cannot return with me when your time comes.'

Suddenly the car seemed quiet and everything seemed so serious. Beth was feeling stifled by this information and it all got a bit too much. Edward sensed this and tried to lighten the mood a little. 'Hey, why don't we skip to the fun bits now, Beth?' Beth's eyes lit up, and he witnessed her beautiful smile once more which seemed to light up the entire car. 'Let's get you out of this car hey,' he said. 'But first you need to learn how to move around a bit in your new state.' He told Beth to close her eyes and visualise herself being sat on the front passenger seat of the car. Beth followed his instructions and she soon found herself sitting in the front of the car.

'That is bloody amazing, Edward!' said Beth excited now at being able to manoeuvre this strange body of hers.

'Great work, Beth!' laughed Edward. 'Now practice a bit more moving around inside here until you feel really confident with it,' he demanded. Beth didn't need telling twice and she shut her eyes tightly and visualised herself being in the driver's seat, then on the back seat of the car and then returning to the front. Edward followed suit in a kind of cat and mouse chase around the interior of the vehicle.

Once Edward felt assured that Beth could now move around the car with ease, he decided it was time to help her step outside. 'This is a little trickier to get used to,' he said as Edward put his body through the door at the rear of the car. Beth just watched in awe as his body appeared on the outside of the window with Edward cheekily waving his hand at her.

'Oh shit, that looks scary,' Beth shouted at him.

Edward then pushed his body back through the door and was sat beside Beth on the back seat. 'I can't do that,' Beth exclaimed.

'Of course, you can, it just takes a bit of practice, that's all.'

Beth positioned herself next to the door and found herself pushing her shoulder into the upholstery. She felt a weird sensation almost like a tingling all over her body and then she looked down at her arm which was on the other side of the door dangling in the fresh air. 'Oh God, I'm actually doing it!' she shouted laughing at the same time.

'That's it Beth, keeping going and you will soon be through,' replied Edward. Beth followed his advice and pushed and pushed. She found herself on the pavement outside the blue car and standing on her two feet for the first time in what seemed like an eternity. The air felt different as it swept across her skin, and there was an eerie intenseness to the atmosphere, which made Beth want to get back inside the car. She leant into the car window and found herself back on the seat next to Edward. 'Good effort,' he said. Beth was just glad to be back in her secure and small space.

'Okay, Beth, time to travel outside and get you to the local police station,' Edward directed.

'Do we have to go now, it's dark?' replied Beth.

'Afraid so, Kiddo, as time is not on our side. Now let's just get outside again on the pavement before we move on to the cop shop, okay?' Beth nodded reluctantly and they both pushed through the walls of the car. As Beth became accustomed to her legs once more, the two youngsters began walking towards Hyde Town Centre. There were not many people out on the streets and what noise was heard came only from the cars that were speeding past in both directions. Beth walked close to Edward feeling uncomfortable in this strange, but at the same time, familiar world.

It just doesn't have the same feeling anymore, Beth thought. It felt like she was in a dream, a nightmare, in fact, one from which she would never be able to wake up. The odd person they passed on the walkways seemed to pass by unaware of their presence, just like Brian in his car. Beth found that truly surreal. She tried not to stray her vision, keeping her eyes focused in front, as she was afraid of what she might glimpse in the pockets of shadows where the street light could not reach. In the background amongst the dark, were in fact peering eyes that were following Beth along the streets. They could see a thin, silver thread attached to her body which extended further the more she walked away from her safe zone—the car.

'Wow, things have certainly changed around here,' said Edward. He felt similar to Beth; this place was strangely familiar to him, but unknown at the same time.

The shop fronts were in the same place as Edward remembered them to be, but with different frontages, bright dazzling signs and they were selling different stuff. The cars were a lot faster than he recalled in his lifetime and they looked a lot smaller and more modern. There seemed to be a lot more people drifting up and down the streets who were wearing odd clothes. 'It must be difficult for you being back here,' said Beth.

'It's okay,' Edward replied. 'I don't feel anything sad or bad. I just feel amazed about how it's all changed, that's all. The girls are even prettier now,' he laughed as three young teenage girls came out of the local off-license and past them in the street. Edward could not believe his luck. These girls were walking about with hardly any clothes on and it was bloody winter. 'I could get used to this,' he grinned.

'Come on, Casanova,' said Beth as she quickened her pace. As she walked past the shop windows, she caught a glimpse of something across the street. The figure appeared to descend back into the brickwork, and Beth felt a nervous shiver go up her spine. 'Did you see that?' she asked.

Edward was oblivious as he was enjoying his walk a little too much and appeared to be gawking at all the girls. 'What?' he replied.

'That weird thing across the road,' said Beth.

Edward stopped and peered across the street to the row of terraced houses. He looked cautiously up to the slated roofs and down the blackened side alleyways. He saw nothing. 'Come on, Beth, let's keep moving.'

Beth and Edward walked casually down the long street leading into Hyde Centre. The night was cool, and there was a small ray of faint mist falling from the clouds that were trying to rain. A dark shadow that was hiding in the backstreets noticed a gleaming silver thread coming from this young girl's body, which stretched out longer with every step she made. This particular lost soul knew that the master would be very happy to hear of such news and so he scurried back to the graveyard in haste. When he reached the large tree, he saw the master and some other souls seated on the grass. He rushed over to tell the news. 'Master, I have seen something truly amazing tonight,' he said.

The demon beckoned him closer. 'Tell me, my dear, what did thou see?'

The poor soul was of a young boy who was eager to please his master. He began to tell his tale. 'I saw a young girl and boy walking down the street tonight but they appeared different to all the rest.'

The demon's attention heightened as he began to stand. 'Tell me, boy. What do you mean when you say they were different?' he replied, smiling and turning all of his attention on to the boy.

'Well, Sir, you could see through them as they walked down the street and it was as if no one else could see them but me.'

The demon grinned and asked, 'Where do you think they were going?'

'I do not know, Sir, they were headed into the town centre but I knew you would want to know so I left straight away to tell you.'

The demon knew these were fresh souls as he called them. Fresh souls belong to human bodies that have just died. They do not remain here for long and usually pass over into the afterlife. It was very interesting that these two young people were still walking around on the Earth plane. The boy suddenly remembered the silver thread and told his master. The demon now knew this was from a soul that had not crossed over as yet. He knew he had to get to this soul and that this would help him in destroying his master for good. If he could only possess this soul and maybe enter the afterlife through her. The thought of the destruction he could cause was almost too much for the demon. He picked up the young boy and spun him around and around laughing as he said, 'Thank you, my boy, you have made me very happy indeed.'

14

Harry concentrated with all his strength as he carefully studied each photograph looking for some recognition of the blue car he kept seeing in his mind. He clutched Beth's small crystal in his right hand and felt the stone throb against his warm skin. 'Come on, Beth, give me something here, what kind of car was it? I need a number plate or make of car, come on, girl, let me see it,' he said to himself.

He flipped back and forth between two images, and suddenly he had a clear vision in his mind of the second image which showed a Ford Cortina with a second image flashing a series of letters and numbers. 'Shit!' Harry shouted, 'I've got it.' He ran from the room gripping the photograph and headed to the intelligence room. George was stood at the wall studying every piece of evidence now written up next to the girl's photographs. 'I've got it, George,' Harry shouted as he ran into the room. George turned around fast, and Harry handed him the photograph, 'It's a brand new Ford Cortina George, and what's even better is I've got some of the bastard's number plate!'

The two men grabbed each other's arms and bounced up and down in front of a group of stunned uninformed onlookers. George quickly wrote up the make and model of the car on the wall and ordered two police officers to get to work on checking all owners of Ford Cortinas over the past few years. Meanwhile, more bodies were gathering in the large room ready for the meeting to recap on the day's further investigations.

15

Brian had been feeling rather triumphant over the past few days with the hidden knowledge of his latest sacrificial maiden safely placed at the back of his mind. After work, he ate and changed into his gardening attire to attend to his allotment. It was dark and cold as Brian walked around his patch of well-toiled earth. The flowers were still rich in colour despite the tepid light from the moon and artificial lights surrounding the plot, they seemed to spread their warmth on the autumn night. Brian checked his vegetables and with a satisfied smile on his face turned to walk towards his humble wooden shed.

Safely inside his refuge, Brian sat in his well-worn but highly comfortable armchair. He delayed turning on his cassette player and just laid back his head and closed his eyes. For Brian, reminiscing about his latest fete was almost as intoxicating as the kill. Oh, how he loved to go over every fine detail in his head. He could feel an erection already just by visualising picking up his last victim that early evening, in his car. *Oh pretty maiden, you were certainly the prize. Spirited no doubt; but you were no match for your master? Fate guided me to you, and I treasured your soft, smooth baby skin and when I entered you I felt ecstasy, my dear. Your small perky breasts; oh how I enjoyed sucking and caressing them, oh you certainly were my favourite and what a stunning offering to the Earth.* Brian relieved himself once more and then got up to make a cup of strong tea. He sat back down and turned his music on. He felt the urgency come over his entire body while the dark melody raged around in his head. *Tomorrow,* he thought, *fate will come knocking once more.*

16

Beth and Edward found themselves on Clarendon Road in Hyde outside a large, rectangular redbrick building filled with blue-rimmed windows. In front of this was a smaller structure with an unusual cylinder shape made out of thick square glass tiles. At the top of that construction was a blue funnel-shaped roof with a small sign reading Hyde Police Station. Edward asked Beth to visualise herself inside the station and with that, the pair reappeared inside the main entrance. They made their way through to the back of the building and could hear lots of noise coming from a large room to their right. Beth entered the room first, and immediately her eyes were drawn towards the large wall full of images and inscriptions. She walked slowly towards the front of the venue and stood in front of one of the photographs staring at it intently. 'That's me,' she pointed out to Edward. 'Oh my God, Eddie, that's a shocking photo of me, I look such a dork.' Edward had caught up and observed the images and information. He said nothing. Beth turned her attention to the other pictures showing pretty girls around the same age. She looked at the dates and said, 'I told you, Ed, this bastard has killed these poor girls too, I knew it.'

'Yeah, and within the last year,' added Edward.

Beth scoped the entire wall and turned to Edward. 'It looks like they've got nothing on him so far, Ed.'

Edward reviewed the content on the wall and read a few dates and details but there was no mention of a description of the man or any witness statements. 'You're right there, cuz,' he replied turning his attention to two men who were stood in front of him and Beth who were asking for everyone's attention. Edward motioned Beth to the side of the room so they could hear what the men were talking about.

George and his sidekick Detective sergeant John Mason began. 'Okay, let's get started, thanks to our very own Harry, we now have the make and model of the car we think is involved in this case and what's more, Harry has given us some letters and numbers that may be connected to the killer's number plate.'

The whole room cheered with Beth and Edward turning towards each other with looks of awe on their faces. *This was great news now they could arrest this bastard,* thought Beth.

'What information have we on that?' asked George looking at the two guys he had ordered to check earlier.

'Sir, the make is a Ford Cortina, Mark V, a 4 door saloon, and if we use Harry's letters and numbers, it looks like it may have been released in January this year, Sir.' The man continued, 'We have over a hundred new vehicles purchased within the metropolitan district which we are checking into at this minute, Sir.'

George replied, 'Good work, Scot, but I want the names of the people who bought this car this year, on my desk by tomorrow, do I make myself clear?'

Constable Scot Berrick was already exiting the room, as he shouted, 'Yes, Sir, I'm on it.'

George continued, 'Any updates on the missing girls?'

Someone from the back of the crowd of officers stood up and replied, 'No, Sir, we cannot find any connections between the girls despite checking all their friends, employment and school records. We even checked their medical and dental records but couldn't find anything.'

John took over at this point, 'Any further information from the work on the ground?' which was all the officers they had spare who had been going door to door to find out if anybody saw anything on the days prior to the missing victims.

A small, blonde haired constable stood up and cleared his throat before he replied, 'Sorry, Sir, we got nothing.'

'That's bloody well right, you've got squat,' said Beth. She scanned her eyes around the room to witness other people beginning to enter. There were about five of them, and they hovered around the edge of the crowd. She noticed they were dressed in plain clothes, unlike the uniformed attire that made up most of the occupants. Their clothes appeared all tattered and ripped. She quickly scanned some of their faces, and they all looked like they were sleepwalking, with no emotions shown upon their pale faces. She caught one of the female figures turning in front of the main wall, and suddenly Beth caught her gaze.

Beth shrank back into the safety of the crowd as when she looked into the women's eyes, Beth had seen pure terror. She got Edward's attention and pointed to the almost floating figures on the outskirts of the room. 'We don't have much time,' Ed said urgently. 'We really need to get you back to the car, Beth.'

'Let's go,' demanded Beth as she eyed the door.

Just as they were leaving Beth stopped in her tracks as she saw George and John both applaud as a tall man with scruffy looking hair, wearing a cool pair of converse sneakers stood up in front of the crowd. 'Here's the man of the hour, our very own psychic Harry!' George shouted with everyone in the room now standing up, cheering and clapping.

Harry felt awkward and blushed. 'Thanks, but I didn't do much really,' he said.

Beth walked across to Harry and replied, 'You can say that again, psychic my arse! Come on then, if you're so fucking psychic why can't you see me?' Beth was almost nose to nose with Harry by this stage, and she had forgotten the creepy ghost-like figures swirling around the outer reaches of the well-lit room. Harry stepped backwards and nearly lost his balance. He couldn't believe it, he had heard every word Beth has just spoken, however; he couldn't see anything.

'Hey, I heard that, and what is it I'm supposed to have done or not done?' Harry replied sternly, as he felt somewhat insulted, but wasn't quite sure why.

Both Beth and Edward jumped in bewilderment, as they realised what had just happened. Beth used the moment instantly. 'You can actually hear me then, Harry?' she replied.

'Yes,' Harry confirmed as he quickly starting walking towards the door. Talking to dead people was one thing but not in front a bunch of so-called sceptics, they'd think Harry had gone completely mad. Harry found an unused interview room and closed the door behind him. 'Now, what is it I can help you with,' Harry began.

Beth and Edward did not know where to start. 'My name is Beth Cotten,' Beth said. *Better to start at the beginning,* she thought. 'It's a long story but I am here with my uncle Edward, who has also passed away. Ed died in the 1960s. He's been sent to help me, as I need help in catching the person who killed me and I think he is the same person who killed all those over girls as well.' Beth paused and tried to contain her excitement.

'Hi, Harry, I'm Ed,' Edward quickly chimed in.

'Hi, Edward, nice to meet you or hear you I guess,' grinned Harry.

'What can you tell me about this man?' asked Harry.

'I don't know his name but he does have a blue Ford Cortina, and he picked me up in it on the night I died. He offered me a lift into Stalybridge and I was running late, so I got in. I know it was stupid of me,' Beth exclaimed.

'Do you know anything else about him that we can use to help the police track him down?' asked Harry.

Beth looked at Ed, and they both looked confused. Ed suddenly shouted out, 'He lives on Cedar Lane in Hyde.'

'Yes,' agreed Beth. 'Number 1 Cedar Lane, I think,' she added.

Harry was finding it hard to contain his exhilaration. 'That's brilliant, anything else? What about a description of the man?' Beth gave a full description of Brian Middleton and Harry wrote it all down. Soon Beth could see dark shadows appearing underneath the door and heard strange noises, almost like weak moans and whispers. She looked at Ed who knew exactly what she meant. Edward explained to Harry that they had to leave now, but they arranged to meet up at Cedar Lane the next day. Ed told Beth to quickly visualise being back in Brian's car. Seconds passed and they found themselves sitting on the backseat of the Blue Ford Cortina parked up on Cedar Lane. 'Why didn't you tell me I could do that before?' said Beth. 'I would have preferred not to have taken that walk in the first place.'

'Thought it would have been fun for you,' Edward smirked.

Meanwhile, Harry was left alone in the small room staring at his notebook, thinking how on Earth am I going to explain this to George?

17

Ava and Angela devoured a homemade potato and leek soup with a small, fresh bread roll that Ava had made the night before. 'You are an amazing cook,' Angela said with half her mouth filled with juicy soup and a mouthful of crusty white dough.

'I'm glad you appreciate it, Ang; at least someone likes my food,' replied Ava.

'Have you thought any more about how to get some money out of that creepy husband of yours?' Angela said.

'No, I can't think of anything convincing.'

The two women finished the rest of their lunch and then Angela lit up a cigarette.

'You know you are entitled to that money Ava, you work just as hard as he does.' Ava nodded but thought Angela really didn't understand what Ava was dealing with. Brian appeared polite and charming on the outside, but only Ava knew what he was truly capable of, and she had the scars to prove it. 'What about that number I gave you? Have you contacted them yet, Ava?' Ava had no need to answer as the look on her face said it all. 'What are we going to do with you? Angela replied. 'Why don't you just come and stay with me and my sister?'

Ava pondered over her choices before replying. 'There is nothing more I would like,' she said. 'But you don't know him, he would cause you and your sister so much trouble, and I couldn't live with that. You are the only friend I have in the world, Ang, and I don't want anything bad to happen to you.'

'We would be okay, Ava, we could tell the police, and he would have to leave us all alone.' Ava wondered about that.

'I'll try to ask him tonight for the money,' Ava promised.

18

Ava tensed as she heard footsteps coming down the hallway. She knew there was no way she would ever pluck up enough courage to ask him for the money. Brian strolled into his kitchen and pecked Ava on the cheek. 'Good Morning, Ava,' he said cheerily. Ava knew when Brian was in this kind of mood; it could mean a pleasant morning or turn out to be a nightmare. Ava shivered, as she smiled at Brian who was now making himself a cup of coffee. Today was Brian's unofficial day off, as he had told his boss the previous night that he wouldn't be able to make it in today. He came up with a story related to Ava's health and the boss told him to take the week, if he needed it, without even blinking an eye, as Brian had a reputable work history with the company and hardly any sick time to his name. Ava was unaware of his plans, but that was no different than most days. She would go to work and come home to an empty, bland house where Ava would automatically prepare the evening meal. If Brian was at home, he would often eat his meal in front of the TV or sit in the kitchen with her, which Ava hated more. If Brian was late home, as he often was these days, the plated meal would be placed on a pan of hot boiling water with another plate on top to keep the food hot. Ava checked the time, grabbed her coat and handbag and said her goodbyes. Five minutes later she was walking down the road to catch her daily bus to Hyde Town Square.

Brian also grabbed his coat and pulled a small black notebook out from his briefcase and closed the front door. Beth and Edward were settled in the back seat when they noticed Brian approaching the car. Beth automatically cringed and slid down the back seat hidden from view whenever she saw him, before remembering that he could not see her. Once in the car Brian turned up the music and rolled out of the street with a strange contentment written all over his face. 'He's up to something, I can tell,' Beth said to Edward who was now eyeing up Brian's small notebook on the passenger seat.

'Yeah tell me about it, Beth, he isn't wearing his usual work stuff, and he seems to be going in a different direction this morning.'

'What are we going to do? We said we would meet Harry here and we can't let him down, but I want to see what he's up to,' said Beth with a puzzled look on her face.

'I know!' Edward replied.

'You stay here to meet Harry, and I can stay in the car and find out what he is up to.'

'Remember, Beth, you only have a few hours with Harry then you must imagine yourself back to this car, okay?' Beth nodded and disappeared.

She waited at the lamppost opposite the killer's house and focused on the white door. Beth couldn't get the images from last night out of her head. The strange looking figures that were floating in that room at the station. She forgot to ask Edward who they were, but she had a good idea that she knew already. She remembered Edward mentioning the "lost souls". Perhaps it's them? She didn't want to look around the street in case she saw them again; even in broad daylight, they made her feel uneasy.

19

Harry slowly moved away from the table and made his way back to the intelligence room. He approached George who was in discussion with a few constables. 'Guv, can I have a quick word with you in your office?' Harry indicated.

'Sure, Harry, come with me,' replied George feeling a little intrigued about Harry's serious face. The two men walked across the room to the back of the station and entered George's office where he swiftly closed the door. 'Okay, Harry, what's this about?'

Harry hesitated then spoke. 'You may not believe what I am going to say right now, George, but promise me you won't think I've lost my marbles!' George nodded. 'Well,' Harry began. 'Just spit it out man, for God's sake,' replied George now growing in impatience at Harry's reluctance.

'I met the last victim earlier on and she has her dead uncle with her. She told me that the guy who killed her is called Brian Middleton and he lives at Number 1 Cedar Lane in Hyde, and yes, he drives a new navy blue Ford Cortina.' Harry paused to assess George's reaction. He found George's mouth fully agape with George reaching for his bottle of whiskey in his desk drawer.

'I think I'm going to need a drink, Harry,' he uttered as he poured the liquid into a crystal glass. George gulped most of it down before steadying himself. 'Look, Harry, I know you are one hell of a psychic but shit me; are you telling me that the ghost of the last victim, Elizabeth Cotten, was here in this police station and talking to you?' George appeared flabbergasted. 'I mean it's not that I don't believe you, Harry, it's just well fucking unbelievable.'

'I knew you wouldn't believe me and you think I'm bonkers,' replied Harry.

'No, it's not that,' George replied. 'It's just well, fucking crazy,' he said whilst laughing.

Harry had to agree and burst out laughing after seeing the funny side of it all. When they both recovered, George looked up at Harry. 'Look, I don't know how I will explain this to the boss but if you have any information that's going to get that prick who's killed those poor young girls, then I'm going to give it my best shot, I promise you that,' George said.

Harry felt relief come all over his tense body and continued. 'Guv, that's great, but how are we going to use this in court? I mean evidence from a ghost; we both know it wouldn't stand up in court.'

'Leave that to me,' said George.

20

It was a sunny morning in Cheshire, which wasn't too unusual for September and Brian felt good. He was driving around local streets in his new Cortina which was his pride and joy. He accelerated smoothly and felt the pulsing power behind the 2.0-litre engine.

Moving in and out of his gears, Brian felt completely alive. He surveyed the pavements looking for his next victim. 'Oh, how sweetly divine thou art, oh sweet fate, show me a sign,' he said softly while smiling mercilessly. Hazel Jackson was walking down Victoria Road. She was a tall, skinny girl around Beth's age and she had pitch-black hair which was flowing below her shoulders in the light breeze. Her skin was fair, and she had pretty features with dark eyes. She was dressed in a pair of blue jeans and wore a lime green woollen jumper that fell to her knees. Hazel was unemployed at the moment and was heading to the bus stop having to make her weekly trip into Hyde Centre to sign on "the dole". She hated not having any money but just couldn't seem to hold down a job.

Hazel wasn't that smart, but she had enjoyed school even though she left without any proper qualifications. Hazel loved children and was going to ask the dole officer about any childcare courses she could do. She was feeling enthusiastic for a change and didn't even notice the blue Cortina parked a few hundred yards behind her. Brian was furiously writing in his notebook, adding time, date and using code words to describe his next prize. He carefully hid his car away from the normal flow of traffic on Victoria Road which was busy at most times of the day as it was one of the main roads that took patrons either to Hyde or Ashton Town Centres. He found a small street entrance down from where Hazel was waiting at the bus stop. Tucked away safely enough, but giving Brian a clear viewpoint of the girl.

Edward felt an uneasiness rising in his gut, and he had to restrain himself with all his might from trying to strangle the monster sat in front of him. Not that it would have done much good, as Edward knew, there was no way he could really harm that scumbag, but the feelings he had were so real. *Jesus, Beth, hurry up and get here; I need you. This freak is really too much, and we have to figure out a way of stopping him from killing again. Hurry up, Beth, Please!* Brian felt an incredible urge that was so intense he could hardly breathe. He knew that it was foolish to even think about approaching his next prey especially so soon after his last sacrifice. He continued to fix his dark, cold eyes on Hazel. Brian finally gave in to his cravings and turned on the engine. Edward's body swerved unexpectedly, as Brian pulled out of the quiet nearby street and joined Victoria Road. *Oh, shit; the bastard is going to stop and pick her up! Fuck! What should I do!* It was too late; Brian pulled in at the bus stop and wound his passenger side window down.

Hazel approached with a dull look on her face asking, 'Can I help you?'

'I was just wondering where you are off to?' replied Brian, in his best casual and friendly tone.

'Oh, I'm just going into Hyde and waiting for the bus,' replied Hazel un-phased by Brian's remarks.

'Well, I'm going into Hyde to pick up my wife from work, would you like me to give you a lift?' Brian said. Hazel thought for a moment and realised she was tired of waiting for the stupid bus. She scanned Brian over quickly looking for any signs that he would be a psychopath—whatever Hazel assumed they would be, and having found the man in the blue car to be identified as okay, Hazel nodded. She opened the passenger side of the car and slid on to the seat. She pulled the door shut and fastened her seat belt.

Brian took his time indicating to pull out back onto the busy road and gave Hazel a reassuring smile. Edward was frantic in the back seat and could not believe what he had just witnessed. *Holy Shit! He's going to kill this girl, and there's not a damn thing I can do, Oh, Beth, please come now, I need you.* Edward found himself screaming at the girl in the front seat, 'Get out! He's going to kill you!' Of course Hazel heard nothing.

21

Beth waited patiently at the lamppost outside Brian's home secretly wishing Harry to be there. Before long, a small blue Mini pulled up, and a tall, lean man appeared from the driver's side of the vehicle wearing a long brown coat, pinstriped trousers, white T-shirt and red converse sneakers. His hair was ruffled, and Beth fell in love with the big dimple on his chin. Harry could not see Beth, but he heard her very clearly. 'Hello, Harry! About time too,' she said.

'Oh, hello, Elizabeth, sorry I'm late the traffic was mad,' Harry replied hesitantly.

'That's okay. I'm just joking with you, Harry.'

'So, is this where the guy lives?'

'Sure is, Harry, let's take a closer look,' Beth said already taking steps up the paved walkway towards the front door.

Harry followed unbeknown to him as Beth was invisible to his view. He peered through the front window and could see a reasonably furnished front room in shades of pale green and cream. The furniture was expensive, and Harry could see all the mod cons including the top of the range television and record player. There were two plush sofas and one armchair positioned next to the window with a large brass lamp perfectly situated on top of a small wooden side table. 'This person has great taste,' he said out loud.

'Harry, we're not here to check out the interior design of the place.' Harry smiled and took his focus to the back of the room trying to see if there was anyone in sight.

'Do we know if this guy is living with anyone?'

'No idea,' replied Beth who was now heading around to the back of the building.

'Let's take a look at the back of the place and see if there is a better view,' she said.

Harry followed suit. At the back of the bungalow, Harry and Beth saw a green painted wooden door, and there was another window which they both stared into. Harry could see a clean and modern kitchen with a small round dining table in the middle. There was a vase of freshly cut flowers on the table along with place settings for two. 'This guy looks like he has a wife,' said Harry.

'How could anyone live with that freak?' Beth answered.

'I know what you mean, but the place is too tidy and what man has fresh flowers in the house?' said Harry confidently.

'Are you going to break in and see if you can find any evidence, Harry?'

'Are you joking, Beth, I could get caught, and we have no idea whether there is someone in there or not. Anyhow, I have spoken to the boss, and he's going to look into it; best not to get in the way.'

'But, Harry, both you and I know that your boss doesn't really believe a word you told him, I mean who would, a ghost telling you that she knows who killed her. It sounds crazy and is crazy, Harry!' Beth felt a wave of sadness run over her and Harry knew she was right.

'Listen, Beth, I'm here to help you, and I promise I will. We need to find out more about this guy before I can. I'll come back later to keep an eye on him and watch the house to see who comes and goes.'

'Sounds like a plan, Harry, I have to get going anyway as Edward told me not to be here too long.'

They walked back to the street, and Harry got in his car. 'I'll be back around four, and I'll park up the street out of sight.' 'Okay, Harry, we will find you.' As soon as Harry was out of sight, Beth visualised herself back in Brian's car.

22

Hazel knew instantly that something was wrong as Brian did a U-turn in the middle of the road heading in the opposite direction to Hyde Town Centre. 'Hey, mister, you're going in the wrong direction, Hyde is back that way,' she said nervously. Brian said nothing and knew he would have to shut her up soon before she started to panic, which could be dangerous for him whilst driving a moving vehicle. Hazel felt sick in her stomach and began to shake. She could feel a huge screaming sensation travelling up towards her throat that was ready to roar. 'I think I'm going to be sick, mister, you better stop the car and pull over.'

'Fuck,' shouted Brian, 'not in my new car you fucking bitch!'

With that, Brian swiped his left fist outwards hitting Hazel in the temple. She flopped to one side, and Brian continued driving.

'Shit, I don't fucking believe this,' said Edward who was cringing in his seat. 'Beth, where are you?'

Suddenly Beth appeared on the back seat next to Edward, and she could not believe what she saw. There was a young girl unconscious in the passenger seat, and the bastard was driving towards Stalybridge. 'Oh, Edward, what's happening?' she cried.

'He's going to kill her, Beth,' replied Edward.

'What can we do, Ed? Can you do something?' Edward knew of a few things, but he had never tried them before.

'Listen to me, Beth, I think we can try something, but I'm going to need your help, okay?'

'Tell me quickly, before he stops the car.'

Edward knew that if he concentrated really hard that he may be able to move items in this world. He knew he could not touch a human or deliberately cause harm, but he was sure he could intervene in such circumstances. 'Listen, Beth, I want you to put all your attention on the front windscreen with me. I want you to picture the glass breaking, got it?' he said sternly.

'Yes, Ed, okay, let's do it,' replied Beth already in position staring at the large sheet of glass.

'Okay, after three. One, two, three.' Both Edward and Beth faced the windscreen and envisioned the glass slowly beginning to crack around the edges. Brian was unaware of the small slithering slits beginning to appear in the glass. His mind was on getting to his location and getting his car safely out of sight. Brian's thoughts drifted to what he would do to this young maiden once safely tucked away within the camouflage of the autumn trees. He already had an erection and could feel his groin throbbing in anticipated pleasure.

The kinks in the glass around the edges began to build and spread across the screen, Edward and Beth continued focusing with all their strength. Brian noticed a crack, but by the time he had, the front windshield disintegrated in front of him. The wind blew ferociously into the moving vehicle with Brian's attention lost and Brian finding himself fighting to see. He managed to slow down, and cars were blasting their horns as they sped up and passed by. He pulled on the brakes and stopped beside the curb. Edward and Beth looked at each other with pride and relief. Brian was disorientated and in shock, but he quickly remembered the girl on his front seat. At that moment, Hazel began to groan and move her head slightly. 'Edward,' shouted Beth, 'she's moving, we've got to get her out of this car or he'll kill her here and now.'

Edward tried to think. 'Let's put our attention on her door and try and get it to open.'

'What about her seatbelt? It's strapping her in,' said Beth. 'Okay, let's start with that.' The pair focused on the seat buckle and imagined it undone. The belt clicked out, and then Edward and Beth focused more on the car door. Soon it opened, and Hazel sluggishly slipped out onto the road. Brian could not believe his eyes. *What the fuck is happening here?* He tried to grab Hazel, but she had managed to pick herself up and stagger to the other side of the road.

Brian leant over and slammed the door shut. He started up the engine and slowly drove away. Edward and Beth saw someone coming to help Hazel as they drifted out of sight. They turned to look at each other, and both smiled. Brian was looking for a motor mechanic on the roadside as he knew he had to get his window replaced before he could go home. He suddenly thought about the girl and whether she would go to the police and if she had a good description of him. Brian felt rage flooding his entire being, and he began to howl and scream. He punched the steering wheel harder and harder until his knuckles bled. He cursed and spat until his throat was hoarse. Edward and Beth just stared and cowered in the back seat. Brian found a small backyard mechanic and eased up to the entrance. He took a few deep breaths and got out of the car. A small man wearing blue stained overalls greeted him. 'Wow, mate, what happened there?'

'Oh, a rock hit my screen and my whole windscreen just shattered,' answered Brian. 'Can you replace it? And today?' asked Brian.

The man paused and replied, 'Well, I can get it done, but it will be a few hours.'

Brian nodded and handed over his keys. He walked further up the quiet street and found a pub. As he sat with a whiskey, Brian mused on the previous events. *How on Earth did that windscreen shatter like that? And how the fuck did that seat belt undo? And the car door? It just opened by itself. I could swear that there was something or someone doing that? What am I saying, there's no fucking way anyone else was there. I need to think quickly, what if that bitch goes to the police? I'll deny it; it's her word against mine.* Brian felt uneasy like his world was about to come crashing down on him. How could he have been so stupid and impulsive like that?

23

Harry arrived back at Cedar Lane at 4 pm sharp. He found a quiet part of the road located next to a row of old wooden sheds. He switched the engine off and pulled back his seat so he could stretch out his legs and wait. Meanwhile, Ava was preparing to finish at work by locking up the drug dispensers and cupboards. Angela had already left, and Ava began to secure the premises. During lunch, she had sworn that she would approach Brian tonight and just come right out and ask for the money for her new car. *He has one, so why can't I?* She thought as she was turning the lock in the pharmacy door. 'Brian always gets what he wants and little old me; well, I'm always at the back of the queue. Well, I'll show you, Brian, I'm not prepared to put up with any more of this shit.' Ava continued to talk out loud feeling her anger rising up in her chest and the adrenaline pumping fast around her body causing her heart to accelerate. She began to physically shake and felt queasy in her stomach. 'Oh Angela, I wish you were here with me now.'

Harry began to yawn and was getting way too comfortable in his car. Suddenly he spotted a middle-aged woman wearing a knee-length camel coat and black trousers, with short greying hair turn the corner onto Cedar Lane. She stopped at the same house Beth and Harry were surveying earlier in the day. 'This could be the wife,' said Harry to himself. His assumption seemed right as Ava turned to walk up the concrete path and reached for her keys to open the white door. *I wonder if she knows what her dearest gets up to*, Harry pondered. His thoughts were interrupted by two hysterical voices shouting Harry's name. The noise seemed to be coming from outside his car, so he wound the window down and listened.

'Harry, holy shit; he's tried to kill another girl, right in front of our eyes,' panted Beth with Edward nodding in agreement unbeknown to Harry.

'Yes, I saw the fucking lot, he spotted her at a bus stop,' cried Edward.

'Yes, just like the fuck must have done with me,' said Beth.

'Wow, is the girl dead?' replied Harry trying to get his head around what he had just heard.

'No, thank God,' replied Beth. 'Edward and I managed to shatter his windscreen whilst he was driving, and we helped the girl get out of his car. She was picked up by someone on the pavement, and the guy just drove off. We left him as he made his way to a garage to get his screen fixed.'

Harry knew he had to calm these two overexcited teenagers down, so he ordered them both to get into the back seat of his car. Once Beth and Edward were safely on the backseat, Harry spoke to them sternly. 'This is all getting out of hand and too much for the likes of us to deal with. I suggest we sit here until you guys calm down and then we will talk about what to do next, okay?' Both Beth and Edward replied with a soft "yes". There was silence for a while, and Harry began thinking about their next move. He knew that the guy would be back soon, and he could not afford to be seen. The murderer would probably be in a rage by now, and they didn't need any more excitement or killings for that matter. 'I'm going to drive us back to the police station and let George know what's just happened. Maybe he can do some digging and find out who this girl is.' Harry started up the engine and drove out of the street.

Ava quickly changed out of her work attire into something more comfortable and began making dinner. She knew that she would have a better chance of talking to Brian if he was fed and watered when he came home. She peeled potatoes and took out two large steaks from the fridge. Ava was a good cook, and Brian knew this. That was one of the main reasons he kept her around. Ava opened a bottle of red wine and poured herself a large drink. She didn't usually drink alone, but she needed something to calm her nerves. Ava continued to chop vegetables straight from the allotment and placed a tray of potatoes covered in olive oil, salt, rosemary and garlic into the hot oven. While the potatoes were roasting, she quickly went to the telephone, which was sitting on a small wooden table in the hallway, and dialled Angela's number. 'Hi, what's up?' said a very chirpy Angela.

'Hi, I just needed to hear your voice that's all,' replied Ava. 'You sound terrible, Ava, maybe you should leave it for tonight until you feel stronger.'

Ava cringed and replied, 'I will never feel strong, Ang; I just have to do it and hope he agrees.'

Angela tried to make Ava feel more relaxed and started telling funny stories about her kids and all the mischief they had got up to. Ava laughed which helped ease some of her tension, but in the back of her mind, she knew Brian would be home soon. 'Wish me luck, sweetheart,' said Ava as she put down the receiver. The smell of the garlic and the fresh potatoes roasting away in the oven reminded Ava of home when her mother was in the kitchen. Ava smiled sadly as she missed her mamma and papa so much. She wished she had never left Croatia. In fact, she wished she had never met Brian.

24

Brian checked his watch and started to walk back towards the mechanics. He was greeted by a younger man in fresh overalls and matching smile. 'Your car is ready, Sir. If you could just come into the reception area where your bill is waiting.'

Brian didn't even acknowledge the young mechanic and strolled boisterously into the main reception. He wrote his signature and paid the woman in cash. 'Nice guy,' said the woman sarcastically as Brian drove off in a hurry.

He couldn't stop thinking about the other woman and how the fuck she had been able to get out of his car like that? *Jesus, I must be losing my mind*, he thought. *What if she's gone to the police and they're waiting at home for me? How am I going to explain this one to Ava? Fuck, we need to get away tonight. Maybe she's too fucking scared to go to the police? Oh, I don't fucking know.* Brian thought some more and knew he had to make Ava tell the police that he had been with her all afternoon since she came home from work. *Yes! That would work. They can't touch me then.*

Brian smelt the roasting potatoes and aroma of cooked meat as he opened his front door. Ava walked quickly down the hallway to greet him with a glass of red wine in her hand. 'Hello, darling,' she said half-heartedly, but Brian's mind was obviously occupied with other things.

'Hello, Ava,' he replied as he grabbed the wine from her hand and downed the whole glass. Ava looked at him in amazement; she had never seen him do anything like that before. Ava knew there was something wrong and retreated back into her kitchen where she thought she would be safer. 'Get me a refill would you, luv?' shouted Brian as he entered their bedroom to change his clothes. Ava quickly poured another glass and placed the food on the dining room table.

I can't ask him now, she thought. *Not while he is in such a foul mood. No, I said I would, no matter what, and I'm still going to ask for the money.*

Brian soon tucked into the hearty meal and gulped large quantities of wine down in between. Ava hardly touched her meal and waited for Brian to place his knife and fork down on his plate. This would mean that she could speak as Brian insisted on silence while they finished their meals. 'Brian, I want to ask you something,' said Ava nervously.

'Go on,' sneered Brian. He knew it would have to be something about money as Ava always started the conversation this way when she wanted something.

'I would like my own car, Brian, as I think it's only fair as I work just as hard as you do and bring home my share of the money. I just want a small reliable car that I can use for work and going shopping and, of course, for going to church each Sunday.' Ava paused and couldn't bear looking up into those beast-like eyes of his.

Brian knew if Ava was to lie to the police for him then he would have to keep her on his side. He pretended to think about it before answering, although he knew he would have to agree now. 'How much are you thinking of?' he replied.

Ava could hardly believe her luck. She never thought the conversation would even get this far and she hadn't even thought about a figure. 'Well, what are small new cars going for these days?' she eagerly replied.

Brian caught the word new and realised he couldn't get away with buying Ava a second-hand car. 'A couple of grand, I think,' he answered coldly.

'Well, then a couple of grand it is,' replied Ava smugly and feeling very confident indeed.

Brian sighed and knew he had no other option than to agree. 'Okay, I will go to the bank tomorrow, and then we can go looking for the kind of car you want.' Ava acted quickly and agreed before Brian could change his mind. Ava knew once the money was brought into the house, she could take it and be free from him forever, or so she thought.

Ava began to clear away the dishes when Brian placed his hand on hers and quietly ordered her to stop and sit down. *Oh, shit, he's going to change his mind now,* she thought.

'Ava, I need to ask you to do me a big favour,' Brian said in an unusually urgent manner.

Before Ava could reply, the telephone began to ring from the hallway. 'I'll get it,' said Ava rushing to the phone. Brian couldn't help thinking who was calling at this time of the evening? As they did not have any acquaintances, well, none that he was aware of anyhow.

Ava picked up the receiver and knew straight away it was Angela. 'Have you done it yet?' said Angela in an excited tone.

Ava knew Brian would be listening and answered, 'Sorry, I think you have the wrong number, goodbye.'

Ava hurriedly replaced the receiver and turned to walk back into the kitchen. Before she had taken her first step, Brian was at her side. 'Wrong number?' he replied.

'Yes, of course,' said Ava, 'who do we know who has our telephone number?' Brian lingered around the phone as if half expecting it to ring once more where he was in prime position to pick up the receiver and witness the voice for himself. Ava walked back into the kitchen and gulped down some more wine; she had a feeling she would be needing its effects shortly. While Brian was stood at the telephone table, he noticed something hanging out of Ava's camel coat that she wore each day for work. He placed his hand inside the pocket and pulled out a business card with the name "Domestic Violence Support" written on the front of it. He turned the card over, and there was a list of telephone numbers and lists of venues where one could go for moral support. Brian put two and two together and knew that Ava was not after a new car, no; she was after the money so she could escape. Today had really been the worst, what with the knowledge that the police may soon be knocking at his door and now this. Ava was planning on leaving him, and Brian was not happy. He looked around where he stood, and his eyes caught the umbrella stand. In the stand were a selection of umbrellas and golf clubs. Brian reached in and pulled out a long, thin metal club. He hid it behind his back as he walked steadily back towards the kitchen and Ava.

25

Rose was in her mid-fifties and very overweight, that's why she and her husband, Carl, were going for evening walks to help them both improve on their health and lose a bit of weight. They had been married for over 35 years and had three grown up children and seven grandchildren. Rose worked at the local bakery, and Carl was a car salesman. They had lived in Stalybridge for as long as they could remember and were well known locally. Each night the couple would grab their rather spoilt cocker spaniel named Polly and walk the streets for at least 30 minutes or until Rose felt her legs ache. Polly had stopped at a lamppost where she excitedly sniffed and panted around. Carl noticed across the road a car windscreen shattering and the driver trying frantically to steady his car. He pulled into the curb and both Rose and Carl noticed the passenger car door swing wide open onto the road. At that moment they could not believe their eyes as they saw a young woman fall onto the tarmac with cars racing past on both sides of the busy road. 'Oh my God, Carl,' cried Rose. 'That poor young lass is going to get splattered all over the road if we don't do something quick.' Before Rose had finished her sentence, Carl had crossed the road and was helping the young woman to her feet, and he quickly guided her safely back to where Rose was standing. 'Oh my poor girl, are you okay?' said Rose. Hazel was still in a daze and was not really sure what was going on.

'Let's take her home with us, Rose,' said Carl. 'She could do with a nice cup of tea; she's in shock the poor dear.' Both Rose and Carl held onto Hazel with Polly walking at their side.

When Hazel had swallowed a cup of warm sugary tea, she began to feel more lucid. She was sat on a comfortable sofa and the fireplace gave off a warm glow. Her head was throbbing and she felt dizzy. Rose had made her comfortable, and there was a plate of chocolate digestive biscuits placed on a small round wooden table next to Hazel's left knee. Polly was lying outstretched on a cream fur rug soaking up the heat. 'Tell us what happened, luv?' said Rose with a concerned look on her face. 'Do we need to call anyone?' asked Carl.

Hazel's voice was soft and hoarse as she uttered the words, 'That bastard was going to kill me.'

Rose looked at Carl and gestured towards the green telephone perched on top of the window sill opposite the fireplace. 'I think we need to call the police,' said Rose.

Carl stood up and approached the telephone dialling 999 as Hazel continued to speak. 'He said he was going to Hyde to pick up his wife and he looked normal,' she cried.

'Yes, luv,' replied Rose and all the time staring at Carl.

Carl got through to the police and provided their address. Rose took hold of Hazel's hands and said, 'Don't be frightened anymore, sweetheart, that was the police and they are coming over here to have a chat with you.'

Hazel carried on telling her story. 'He looked okay so I got in his car and he was driving in the wrong direction. I knew he was not going to take me to Hyde and at that moment I felt so scared.' Hazel began sobbing, and Rose and Carl both put their comforting arms around her. Polly started licking Hazel's hands which made Hazel giggle for a second before she went back to sobbing.

'Can we phone your mum or somebody?' asked Rose. Hazel gave Rose her mum's number and Carl made the call. 'Do you want to tell us what happened next?' said Rose.

Hazel composed herself and said, 'The bastard punched me in the head and then I don't remember anything else until I was on the road.'

'You're safe now, luv,' said Rose. Hazel lay back on the soft sofa and closed her eyes. 'Jesus, Carl, did you get a look at the car or the guy driving it?' said Rose quietly.

'No, luv, it all happened so quickly,' replied Carl. 'I do know it was a Ford Cortina and the new model too,' he uttered. 'The man driving it seemed to be in his mid to late forties, I think, and he was going bald and had dark rimmed glasses on. That's all I can remember,' said Carl.

'I hope they catch that swine before he tries it on another innocent girl,' said Rose.

Soon the police arrived, and Hazel was able to tell her horrific tale again. The police officer took notes and asked Hazel to describe the man. She gave a similar account as Carl; however, she was able to be more specific in terms of the man's clothes and his accent. Hazel complained of an increase in pain around her temple, so the police arranged for her to be reviewed at the local hospital in Ashton. 'You can never be too careful,' said the constable as he escorted Hazel to the police car.

Rose telephoned her mum and told her to go directly to the hospital where she would soon be reunited with her daughter. Hazel squeezed Rose and Carl's hands as she stepped out into the street. 'Thank you both so much,' she said. 'You really saved my life, and I will never forget you.'

'It was our pleasure, luv,' replied Rose as she planted a big kiss on Hazel's cheek. 'Look after yourself now, and don't go taking any more lifts from strangers,' said Carl. Hazel waved from the back seat of the vehicle as it drove out of sight.

26

Harry entered Hyde police station and found George in the incident room gazing at the somewhat beautiful but disturbing photographs of four missing young girls. Harry grabbed George by the arm and asked if they could speak in private. George motioned to his office, and Harry blurted out the events of the day as soon as the office door was sealed shut. 'Look, George, I know this is one hell of a story, and there is no way I can blame you from not thinking I've lost the plot but the guy tried to kill another girl today.' George's eyes opened wider and he urged Harry to carry on with this tale. 'Beth and Edward were both in the back seat of the guy's car, and he picked up a young girl on Victoria Road who was waiting for a bus. Edward said it was spontaneous as the guy started off perving at her and writing notes of the time and location. Edward said he just took off and stopped a few yards down from the bus stop and the girl approached his car, probably thinking it was someone she knew.' Harry continued. 'The girl was going to Hyde to sign on *the dole* and the guy said he was going into the centre to pick up his wife. The girl ended up getting into the car, and when she realised he was going in the wrong direction, she started to panic and he punched her hard in the head, and she fell unconscious. Edward and Beth forced his windscreen to smash which made the guy pull over to the curb and then they helped the girl get out of the car.' Harry took a breath. 'They said he went straight to a local mechanics in Stalybridge.' Harry looked at George's face to gage his reaction. George reached for his whiskey again and poured a large one into his glass and knocked it back in one swift swoop.

'Look, Harry, that information you gave me about the blue Ford Cortina worked out. They found a Brian Middleton who does live at Number 1 Cedar Lane in Hyde Cheshire.'

'That's great, Guv,' replied Harry.

'Yes, it's great, but we don't have anything else on this Middleton to go with, and I can't just arrest him without any evidence,' replied George.

'What about checking if this girl has made a charge against him today, George?' said Harry.

'Where was she abducted?' asked George.

'Victoria Road, in Dukinfield, but the windscreen incident happened on Mottram Road in Stalybridge,' replied Harry.

'Why don't you phone the Stalybridge cop shop and see if it's been chased up?'

Without hesitation, George picked up his telephone and asked to be directed through to Stalybridge police station. He gave the details to the senior officer and waited for a reply. Harry couldn't stand the tension and had to pour himself a glass of whiskey with George directing another with his hands. The two men waited for what seemed like an eternity when George finally started saying "yes" and "I see". Harry was trying to listen to what the voice on the other end of the phone was actually saying, but it was no use, it was too faint. George ended the conversation by saying, 'Okay, let me have all the details today, as I think we have some information to put together on this one.' George put the receiver down and looked at Harry with a huge smile on his face. 'Fuck me, Harry; we may well have this bastard yet!'

'What did they say, George?' asked Harry.

'They said the young girl gave a statement as well as two passers-by at the scene that helped the young girl by taking her back to their place and giving her some hot tea.' George took another gulp of his whiskey and continued. 'They said she described him as being in his mid to late forties, bald with dark rimmed glasses. The by-standers also got a description of blue Ford Cortina, which was a newer model and the guy also got a quick look at the man driving the car too.'

'No fucking way,' said Harry feeling his body shaking from head to toe. 'Can you arrest him now, George?'

'Not so fast, kid,' replied George. 'We can go around there and find out where he was at 4 pm this afternoon, and we can have a brief look at his car, but that's all for now, Harry.' Harry slumped back into the chair and stared at his glass. 'Look, Harry, we need hard evidence before we can get this bastard, I'm sorry it's not what you wanted but it's a start hey!' Harry nodded and seemed lost for words. 'Want to come along?' asked George.

'You bet I do,' replied Harry. 'When are we going?'

George looked at the clock on his office wall and it read 6 pm. 'Give me an hour,' replied George.

Harry couldn't wipe the smile off his face as he headed out back into the incident room. Beth and Edward soon found him and were jumping up and down at the news. 'This is fantastic news,' shouted Beth.

'Hang on a minute, Beth,' said Harry. 'This is just going to be a routine call as we don't really have enough on him yet to arrest and charge him.'

'I know, but it will shake the bastard up a bit,' laughed Beth.

'Yeah, it will give him something to think about too,' added Edward.

Beth suddenly saw in her peripheral view a group of dark shapes entering the building from all sides. She froze, and Edward stopped suddenly. 'You okay, Beth?' he asked.

'It's those weird people again, Ed, I don't like the feeling they give me, and they are in the building again and calling out to me.'

Beth looked horrified and Edward immediately remembered how long Beth had been away from the car. 'Look, Harry, we have to get Beth out of here, so we will meet you at the house.'

'Okay,' replied Harry. 'We will be there in about an hour.'

27

Ava didn't see Brian return to the kitchen, as she had her back to him, standing at the sink. She heard his voice which appeared cold and dark as he uttered, 'You're not going anywhere.'

The next thing Ava felt was a rush of pain to the back of her head, and she woke up on the cold tiled floor. Brian was hovering over her, and she felt the cold droplets of blood running down her neck. 'You think you can put one over me, Ava?' he squirmed. Ava flinched as she saw the blunt end of the smooth metal club come down and hit her once again in the face. She felt her teeth shatter and blood splattered about the kitchen spraying a fine mist of red onto the light coloured tiles and cupboards. Ava passed out, and when she awoke, she found both of her hands behind her back which had been tightly bound to one of the wooden dining chairs. Her head throbbed, and her mouth was swollen with blood still seeping out. Brian sat calmly at the other end of the small dining table as he starred at her distantly. 'How dare you even think of leaving me, Ava,' he grimaced. 'You were nothing when I met you, just a poor Croatian peasant,' he said. Ava tried to sit upright, but she was listless, and when she tried to reason with him, she found her mouth incapable of movement. She sensed something gut-wrenching in the pit of her stomach, and soon afterwards a projectile of vomit erupted from her mutilated lips. 'That's disgusting,' shouted Brian. 'You're fucking disgusting, and you wonder why I never feel like having sex with you.' Brian rose from his chair and walked over to Ava's lifeless body. He swung the club hard, and Ava felt its solidity as it made an impact on her right thigh. Brian swung it again and this time hit Ava across her chest. More vomit protruded and Brian chastised her more. 'You will not be required to go to work from now on,' he ordered. 'Your job is to keep this home running smoothly; you hear me, bitch?' Ava passed out once again. Brian was at that moment disturbed by a knock at the front door. He decided to ignore it as he thought it might be someone selling stuff or doing research. In his frenzy, he had completely forgotten about the possibility of being visited by the local police.

28

George accompanied by another uniformed constable knocked harder on the front door of Number 1 Cedar Lane. Harry met with Beth and Edward and stood at the railings leading to the front door. Meanwhile, inside the house, Brian began to panic as he knew it was the police. He had to think quickly. He wrapped a tea towel around Ava's mouth so she could not make a sound and closed the kitchen door. He looked down at his clothes to check for any spots of blood and scanned his hands; they were clean. He wiped the sweat off his brow and checked his hair in the mirror as he walked to open the door. Brian composed himself perfectly and greeted the two police officers as the door swung open. 'Good evening, Mr Middleton,' began George in his official tone.

After introducing himself and his fellow companion, George asked politely if they could enter Brian's domain. Brian was very courteous and ushered the men into the hallway. Harry followed and George introduced him as an associate. Edward and Beth visualised themselves into the property too. Brian led the party into the living room and closed the door to prevent anyone hearing any moans coming from the kitchen. 'Mr Middleton, thank you for seeing us at such late notice and in the evening. We just have a few questions in regards to a young girl today who was abducted in Dukinfield, who escaped her abductor in Stalybridge at around 4 pm this afternoon.' George paused long enough to check the reaction on Brian's face. Brian, on the other hand, was performing at his best with no hint of disconcert or guilt evident at this point. George continued, 'We have witnesses including the young girl stating that the man who abducted her was driving a blue Ford Cortina. We have reason to believe you yourself, Sir, also own such a vehicle, is that correct?'

Brian replied, 'First of all, I am very sorry to hear that this young girl was traumatised today, and I hope you catch the culprit, officers.' George briefly made eye contact with Harry who by this stage was gaping at the mouth and in awe at seeing how calm and collected this guy was. Brian continued. 'Yes, I do drive a Ford Cortina as do many of the population of Britain, as it's a great car and I have recently updated the model.'

'I see,' replied George. 'Do you mind if we ask you of your whereabouts today at 4 pm, Mr Middleton?'

Brian didn't flinch as he answered. 'Oh yes, I had the day off work today and spent most of it at home. I made dinner for my wife who also works and we ate about 5 pm.'

George verified the information by nodding and asked, 'We don't seem to have met your wife, Mr Middleton, would it be possible to ask her the same question?'

Brian was quick and replied, 'Oh, well, you could but she is in bed, ill with a bad migraine I'm afraid. Perhaps you could call back tomorrow evening when she should be feeling much better.' George thanked Brian, and he escorted them swiftly off his premises. Beth felt strange and cowered behind Harry and Edward as she heard this monster lie through his teeth without flinching. She thought about what he had done to her and to those other poor girls and how she wanted so desperately for him to be caught, that it hurt. Edward told her to get herself outside, and they both breathed a sigh of relief as they stood near Harry's car in the fresh night air.

As Brian closed the door, George turned to Harry and said, 'This bastard will be hard to catch, and we need to do everything by the book, so he can't slip away.' They all scanned the blue Ford Cortina parked directly opposite Brian's house and approached with caution. 'Don't lay a finger on this vehicle,' ordered George. 'We're just going to have a look at the front windshield, that's all.' No one needed any guiding as they peered carefully at the rim around the car's front windshield. They all noticed the fresh rubber seal which had obviously been replaced and the young constable's eyes were drawn to a tiny glittering piece of broken glass. George looked up and stared directly into Harry's gaze. 'The fucking bastard is lying through his teeth; this glass has been replaced, so help me God, and today!'

'What you going to do?' asked Harry as he heard both Beth and Edward yelling, 'Arrest the bastard, George!'

George looked down for a second and replied, 'We are going to do this properly, and first of all, we need to see the girl again and speak to this arsehole's wife. When we have enough evidence, we will get a warrant to search this prick's car and home. We will get the bastard, I promise.'

As George disappeared from view, Harry spoke to Beth and Edward. 'You two okay after that?' he asked.

'Yes, we're fine,' said Edward, as Beth was still worked up and didn't feel like talking. 'What's going to happen now?' asked Edward.

'Not sure,' replied Harry. 'I know they will be back tomorrow to speak to his wife and he might have to go down to the station for an identification parade with the victim.'

Beth suddenly found her voice and said, 'Harry, you got to get in that house tomorrow while he's at work and see if you can find out anything more.'

'You heard what my boss said, didn't you, Beth?' Harry replied.

'I know he said everything by the book, but I am running out of time here, and he's far too clever, they will never catch him at this rate.' Harry knew she was right as he had never seen such composure.

'Okay, I tell you what guys, I'll meet you both back here tomorrow lunchtime and we will see if I can get in there.'

'Oh, thank you, Harry, you're my hero,' replied Beth in a playful manner.

'Speaking of heroes, Harry,' Edward teased, 'Beth has never heard of Roy Orbison; do you have any of his records we could play?'

'Roy Orbison, of course, I do, he's the man,' laughed Harry.

'Well, what are we waiting for, let's go and listen to some tunes,' replied Edward. The three of them arrived at Harry's place and spent a good few hours listening to the likes of Orbison, Elvis, Buddy Holly and the Beatles. While Beth was sat enthralled by the novel sounds, she was hearing Edward whispered into Harry's ear, 'Excuse yourself and go to the toilet.' Harry looked puzzled but did what he was told, with Beth hardly noticing the two of them had left the room. When Edward got

Harry out of hearing reach from Beth, he began, 'Look, Harry, I didn't want to scare Beth anymore then she is already, but I need to talk to you about what's been going on and what she is seeing.' Harry now looked afraid as he replied, 'Well, go on then, spill it, Ed.'

'Since Beth refused to go with Michael, she has put herself in danger.'

'Danger!' replied Harry.

'Yes, she has attracted many souls that we call "lost souls", and they are people or they were people of this Earth plane who, like Beth, for different reasons did not leave when they should have.' Harry said nothing and sat down on the toilet seat. Edward carried on. 'Beth is seeing these lost souls a lot now; they appear as dark shadows, and she knows not to look them in the eyes because I told her it was dangerous if she did.'

'How dangerous are they?' asked Harry.

'I don't know a lot about these things, and there are rules to follow whilst I'm here, but I do know that if Beth stays here much longer, they could destroy her soul and she could end up like one of them, destined to walk this Earth for eternity.' Harry sighed. 'And what's more, I think Beth's time has almost run out, and I am worried that she will not leave until that psychopath is caught. This could mean a lifetime of suffering for Beth, and I don't want to see her go through that.'

Harry thought for second and then uttered, 'We need help. Leave it with me, Ed, and I'll speak to my close friend who might know what to do in this situation.'

Both Harry and Edward re-joined Beth in the living room where they found Beth singing out loud to *Hey Jude*. 'Jesus, Beth, stop please, you're ruining a classic,' shouted Edward.

'Like you two can do any better,' she said. This led to the boys overriding her voice with the lyrics of the famous Beatles song, and it sounded even more ridiculous than before. They all burst out in hysterics of laughter, and Harry was laughing so much he collapsed onto the sofa holding his stomach pleading with them to stop.

Edward finally calmed himself down and told Beth, 'Come on, we better get you back to the car, it's not safe being away for so long.'

'See you tomorrow, Harry,' Beth said, as they left and Harry found himself alone on his sofa exhausted after so much laughing that his cheeks ached. Finally, he settled down. But he could not get the images of the black figures out of his head.

29

As soon as the front door closed shut Brian pressed his tense body up against the cold wood. His mind was racing, and he knew the cops would be back. His attention soon returned to Ava who was injured in the kitchen. '*Stupid bitch, why did you want to go and ruin everything for me? Ungrateful bitch! You have it good here with me, why would you want to leave? I need to fix this and quick.*'

Brian turned the handle on the kitchen door and peered inside. Ava was still draped over the chair and the tea towel was still wrapped around her face. He carefully took off the towel which was by now soaked with blood, and Ava moaned softly. Her face had swollen to an unrecognisable shape with dried blood splattered all over her face and clothes. Brian attempted to wash some of the blood away and found some antiseptic in the first aid kit under the sink. He found some painkillers and urged Ava to swallow them, which she did under extreme force as she could not bear to move her lips. Brian gathered some ice and wrapped it in another tea towel and placed it on her swollen jaw and mouth. Ava kept slipping in and out of consciousness. He carried her up to her bedroom and placed her gently in the bed. He walked back down the hallway and began to clean up the rest of the blood on the kitchen floor and furniture.

It was past midnight before the place appeared as if nothing had happened. Ava's face, on the other hand, would take weeks to heal, and Brian knew the cops would be back to question her tomorrow. *Fuck! What the fuck can I do with her? The bitch has to give them a convincing alibi, or I'm fucked for good.* He marched back into Ava's bedroom where her moaning had become more pungent. He tried to give her more painkillers, but her mouth was completely engorged so that Ava was finding it difficult to breathe. Amongst the moaning sounds, Brian could hear unpleasant gurgling sounds coming from Ava's throat. He sat down next to Ava and held his head in his hands. Brian knew it was useless as the cops would definitely arrest him now, and if that young bitch identified him, they would have enough to search the house and his allotment. He would surely be found out.

Brian knew he had to make a run for it. He grabbed one of Ava's pillows beside her now unidentifiable head and covered her face with it pressing down hard. Ava gave a feeble struggle as Brian stifled her already faint breath. She soon lay motionless, and Brian placed his head on her chest to make sure she was dead. When he was satisfied, he pulled back the covers and wrapped her bruised and battered lifeless body in the bed sheet. Brian then proceeded to dash towards the back door where he wheeled a large green garbage bin into Ava's bedroom. It was well past midnight, but Brian thought it less conspicuous to wheel the garbage bin across the road to his allotment rather than humping a large corpse wrapped in a sheet! He picked the limp body up covered in a pale blue cotton sheet and dropped it head first into the plastic bin. Ava's legs were sticking out of the top so Brian struggled to bend and position them both so he could close the lid. He quickly stripped the bed and put the bedspread and pillows into black garbage bags. He could set fire to these once on his allotment as no one would flinch if they saw a fire burning, as it was a usual occurrence with the gardeners. Although the time was a little off.

He wheeled the heavy bin to the front door and rolled it down the path. The air was prickly, and there was enough light from the street lamps to guide him over the road. Edward saw him first as Beth had her eyes shut and thinking of her parents and Tina; *God I miss you all so much.* Edward called out to her in surprise,

'What's he up to now, Beth?'

Beth opened her eyes to find Brian on his allotment heading to his shed. 'He's just wheeled that huge bin from his house,' Edward exclaimed. Beth just stared. 'We better go and see what he's doing,' replied Beth.

Both Edward and Beth positioned themselves outside the wooden shed awaiting Brian's next move. A few seconds later Brian opened the shed door holding a large plastic bag which was full of his small notebooks which he had collected over the series of murders he had performed. He knew this would be enough to send him away forever and he intended on destroying them all tonight before he escaped. He also had a small trinket box, which was full of photographs of the innocent girls before, during and after their demise. Brian walked over to a small area of the allotment where there was no vegetation. There was a small hole where someone had scraped all the soil out of and in the centre was an old rusty metal dustbin. Brian threw the notebooks and pictures into the container and covered it with dry twigs and leaves. He poured some petrol into the bin and lit a match. The fire burned instantly with a waft of grey smoke billowing out into the dark night sky. Brian wasted no time and quickly started digging at the end of his exquisite flower beds. He carefully removed several rows of beautiful coloured flowers and laid them to the side with care. Beth looked at Edward and whispered, 'What's he burying in there?'

Meanwhile, Brian dug through the cold, damp soil in a frenzy stopping at times, only to wipe the sweat from his brow and catch his breath. Beth and Edward watched his every move with dread and intrigue. Brian lay down the shovel and wheeled the garbage bin up to the edge of the now large gaping hole in the earth. He opened the lid and then tipped the enormous plastic vessel on its side. He dragged the wrapped corpse out clumsily and rolled it into the dark pit. Edward and Beth could not believe their very eyes. 'Shit, he's burying what looks like a body,' cried Edward. Beth was paralyzed. 'That's why the girls' bodies were never found, Beth; the bastard has used his flower beds as their graves.' Edward just remembered what he had said and turned to Beth who was by now sobbing and pacing frantically along the line of flower beds. 'Beth, I'm so sorry, that was so insensitive of me. Are you all right?'

Beth shouted to Edward, 'We need Harry now, go and get him, Ed, and I'll keep an eye on this fucker to make sure he doesn't make a run for it.

'But, Beth, will you be okay here by yourself? Edward asked.

'Just go quickly, Ed, we're wasting time,' she said wiping the tears away with the back of her hand.

Edward didn't like leaving her there especially with the dark shapes that could appear at any time, but he knew they really did need Harry. 'Okay, I'll come straight back once I've woken Harry, I promise, Beth, remember, keep a look out for those weird shapes, and if you spot them, get back into the car, you hear me?'

'Yes, just go,' replied Beth.

Once Edward had left Beth's side, the dark shapes began to emerge. They seemed to know that she was defenceless and without anyone to protect her. They entered the allotment and began drifting towards her from all different directions. Beth caught sight of a few of the shapes; they looked like young teenagers with dated clothes as if from a different century. She remembered not to look them directly in the eyes and scanned the large yard for any signs of more. Beth spotted another eerie figure beside Brian who was by now replacing the earth on Ava's makeshift grave. This figure was taller and seemed older, with its dark black hair moving slowly in the light breeze. Two other ghostly figures that looked female were now standing near the fire which was fading, and thick dark smoke engulfed their forms making them both hard to detect. Beth had a really bad feeling rising in her throat, and she knew if she didn't get to the car soon, they would be upon her. She closed her eyes and thought of being safe in the back seat of Brian's car and with that, she opened her eyes and found herself crouched on the floor of the blue Ford Cortina parked outside Number 1 Cedar Lane. Beth made sure that all the car doors were locked and then peered from the rear back window hoping the shapes had vanished. She saw Brian throwing more things into the metal bin and dowsing it with more petrol. Before long, she witnessed large golden flames protruding into the air. The remnants of Ava's bedding. Brian carefully returned the shovel to his shed and wheeled the bin back over the road and around the back of his home to its rightful place. 'Hurry up, Edward,' screamed Beth under her breath. The creepy figures were starting to gather around the fire, and there were even more of them now.

30

Harry woke refreshed and almost jumped out of bed. He was a man on a mission. Oliver curled around his legs as Harry brushed his teeth. 'Hang on, Ollie; you'll get fed in a minute, just wait.' After feeding his best pal, Harry closed the door to his unit and with a piece of toast stuck in his mouth, he climbed into his Mini. Reverend Elizabeth was waiting for Harry as he walked eagerly into the local community centre. She was a serene looking woman and gave the purest smile as she affectionately welcomed Harry to the main table at the front of the empty room. Reverend Elizabeth liked to get to the centre early to bless the room and meticulously prepare the main table with fresh white laid tablecloths, white candles, and an array of healing crystals. 'Hi, beautiful stranger, welcome back,' she said.

Harry grinned from ear to ear and sat down beside her. 'Thanks, Reverend, for agreeing to meet with me,' Harry replied. 'Not a problem, Harry, I am always here for you, I hope you know that.' Harry had a lot to thank Reverend Elizabeth for as she was his main mentor and teacher since he had started to take his psychic abilities seriously. There were still many things Harry did not understand, and he knew he had a long way to go before he reached the skill level of Elizabeth.

'Now, Harry, how can I help you?' gestured the Reverend. Harry clumsily explained the best way he could about the lost souls and Beth's situation. Reverend Elizabeth listened intently only stopping Harry when she needed to know more information. 'Well, Harry,' she replied. 'You have certainly found yourself in an extremely difficult mess! You will need to listen very carefully to me as I try and explain what is going on for that girl and how you may be able to help her.'

Harry poured himself a glass of water from the crystal glass pitcher positioned on the table and drank all of the cool liquid down in one. He suddenly felt anxious and all the hairs on his neck and arms began to stand on end. The Reverend lit the white candles on the table and said a prayer. 'Harry, this is very dangerous stuff we are dealing with, and I need you to protect yourself at all times from now on.' Harry nodded and waited for her to begin. 'These lost souls, as your friend from the other side calls them, are indeed just that. They have walked amongst us for centuries and come from all walks of life. Some may have refused to go into the light, while others may have remained here for unknown reasons. These lost souls individually are relatively harmless to humans and other spirits, however; when they congregate together, they become dangerous. Your friend Beth, is in an unusual predicament as she is about to cross over into the afterlife, however; for the time being she remains on the Earth plane, where her light or soul, attracts the attention of these wandering souls.' The Reverend paused to sip some water. 'Edward told me that they are attracted to Beth because they think that she will be able to take them with her when she crosses over,' stated Harry. 'Is that true, Reverend?' he asked.

'Well, half of that is true, Harry,' replied the Reverend. 'They're attracted to the girl because they see the light of her soul and it reminds them of who they once were so many years ago. They just want to be near the light as they remember the beautiful feelings they once experienced when they too were alive. Sadly, they mean no malicious harm to her, but if they get the chance, they will engulf the poor girl's essence, and she will be drained of all goodness. This will mean that she will remain in the darkness for all eternity, and the girl will definitely be prevented from crossing into the light when her opportunity arises.'

'This sounds so depressing,' replied Harry.

The Reverend smiled kindly and took hold of Harry's hands. 'It's okay, Harry; there is some hope for the young girl.' Harry's face lit up with enthusiasm as the Reverend continued. 'You may not like what I am about to tell you, Harry, but it is best that it comes from me, as I am the best equipped to help you.' Harry did not like the sound of what he was hearing, and he really didn't feel experienced enough in his abilities do this all by himself, whatever it was, he would have to do. 'Harry, I fear that all is not what it seems with this situation,' said the Reverend. Harry froze as he heard these words and braced himself for what he was about to hear next. 'I believe there are other evil forces working with these lost souls, and that is what I am most concerned about,' said the Reverend.

'What evil forces?' replied Harry, who was now shivering and feeling slightly nauseous. He began to pour a second glass of water from the carafe and took no time in gulping down the refreshing fluid which seemed to moisten every inch of his dried out throat. Harry's psychic abilities were more advanced than he liked to think, and he suspected that his adverse physical reactions were testament to the fact that Harry already knew exactly what the Reverend was referring to. Nevertheless, he felt more protected in his current place of denial for now.

'Harry, I believe that there is a demon among those lost souls who is controlling their every move. This creature is the one pursuing Beth for his or its own needs.' Harry's fears had now been confirmed, as Harry had known this before the reverend had opened her mouth to speak. He knew this last night when he could not stop thinking about the black shapes. Harry knew it all right, that is why he had arranged to meet with his mentor, as he knew only she could help him defeat this demon, for Beth's sake. He knew he needed more information and hoped the Reverend could supply this.

'What do you think the demon wants with Beth?' he asked.

'Most demons want only one thing and that is to possess the soul for their own means,' replied Elizabeth. 'Beth is in a powerful position as she is within two worlds at the moment. If the demon can enter her soul, it could wreak havoc on the living or more importantly, it could find its way into the afterlife and destroy the plane by inviting more evil in across the two domains. Either way this would have irreversible consequences to the spiritual world and all of human kind.'

Harry looked across at the Reverend Elizabeth and asked sincerely, 'Can we fix this?' She grabbed both of Harry's shoulders and pressed her fingers hard into his toned muscles before nodding. 'How?' Harry asked.

'First of all, you will need to identify the demon,' replied Elizabeth.

Harry scratched his hair frantically and paused as he heard the word, you! 'Please don't tell me that you won't be there to help me?' Harry pleaded.

'Of course, I will be there, Harry, but you need to do this, and I will be there to guide you,' replied the reverend.

Elizabeth knew Harry was ready for this and that it would give him the confidence Harry desperately needed. 'Okay, how does one identify a demon then?' Harry replied.

'The demon follows the universal rules just like the rest of us and once the demon is identified, it has to show itself.'

'How do you identify a demon?' asked Harry again.

'You need to look the lost souls in the eye and pay attention to your feelings. When you feel a strange haunting feeling in the pit of your stomach and all your hairs along the line of your spine stand on end, and you feel a fear so intense that every fibre of your being wants you to run like hell, then you'll know that you have met the demon by sight, and in turn, the demon will have no choice but to identify itself to you. It's all about your gut feeling and intuition, Harry,' said the Reverend.

'You make it sound easy,' replied Harry. 'How do we get rid of the damn thing?' asked Harry.

'We don't know exactly what the demon will try to do after it is identified. Our main intention is to banish it from the Earth plane for good,' replied Elizabeth. 'We also need to make sure the girl gets to leave in one piece.'

Harry felt totally unequipped for battling against a demon, however; he trusted his mentor completely and knew she would be there to help him if things went wrong.

31

Harry burrowed further down inside his warm bed covers as the night air had begun to change. He felt relaxed, however; Harry was having difficulty falling asleep. He knew tomorrow was a big day where he had to find some answers as Beth's time was running out. He couldn't stop thinking about the black shapes and the demon Reverend Elizabeth had mentioned.

Suddenly he heard Edward's voice shouting down his left ear. 'Wake up, Harry, we need you now, the psycho has just buried someone in his allotment. We think that's where he may have buried the other girls and Beth.'

'Okay, Ed, I hear you, you don't need to make me deaf in the process,' he replied. Harry threw back the covers and shivered.

'Hurry up, Harry, I had to leave Beth at the allotment to keep an eye on him, and she's all alone out there,' said Edward, this time a little quieter.

'Okay, you go back to her, and I will be there as soon as I can. If he drives off in his car, go with him as we can't afford to lose this maniac now,' stated Harry as he desperately shoved his legs into a pair of creased blue pin striped trousers.

'Okay, see you there,' Edward said as he closed his eyes. Harry found a T-shirt and a woollen jumper to help him warm up. He telephoned the reverend, who took a while before she picked up the telephone, but she already knew who it was.

'Okay, Harry, I'll meet you at Cedar Lane, be careful,' she replied placing down the receiver. Harry jumped over Ollie and ran out the door.

Edward arrived back at the car to find Beth cowering in the back seat. 'Oh, thank God, you're back,' Beth smiled with relief. 'Told you I'd be back, kid,' replied Edward who was now checking out the allotment from the window. He couldn't see Brian anywhere in sight, but his eyes were drawn to the group of strange black images converging around the remaining flames of the fire. For now, Beth was safe, but for how much longer, that he did not know. 'Where's he gone, Beth?'

'He took the bin around the back of his house, and I haven't seen him since then.' Beth replied. 'Is Harry coming?' she asked urgently.

'Yes, he's on his way over. He should be here soon.'

'Oh God, what if I am really buried underneath those flower beds, Edward?' Beth started to cry. 'I never thought it would upset me so much, Ed, I mean I thought I was getting used to the idea of being dead, but the thought of it makes my stomach curl and to think that's where I ended up, some life hey?' she sobbed. Edward tried to console her but Beth continued to splutter, 'I really miss my mum, Ed.'

They both jumped when Harry knocked on the car window and grinned his ridiculous smile through the frosted glass. 'About time,' shouted Edward, thinking it would ease Beth's mood. She smiled, and the pair left the car to join him on the pavement underneath the orange light of the lamppost. 'Come on, Harry, we need to find out who else that psycho has buried underneath there,' said Edward.

'You coming, Beth, or do you want to stay in the car?'

'There's no way I'm staying in here on my own, Ed,' she replied. They walked towards the shed and found the shovel resting on the door.

Edward focused on the fire now burning low and noticed the shapes had retreated back for now. 'Come on, Beth, stay close to me though,' he added. Beth walked in front, and they all gathered around the flower bed.

'Where should I start digging?' Harry asked.

'You better see who is in the fresh grave first,' replied Edward,' checking Beth's reaction. Beth nodded and stood as close as she could to Edward whilst Harry began burrowing his way through the freshly returned earth. He soon came to the pale blue cotton shrine at the top of the grave. He gently unwrapped the sheet to discover the horrific site of Ava's distorted head.

'Oh fuck,' cried Harry.

'What is it?' asked Edward peering closer to the side of the grave. He too caught sight of the dreadful image of a women's face that had been brutally mangled. Edward quickly turned to

Beth and stood in her path so Beth could not lean over to see this sickening image.

'Let me see,' cried Beth impatiently.

'No, Beth, this is not something you need to see, please just stay where you are,' motioned Edward.

Beth unwittingly did as Edward suggested. 'I think it's the guy's wife but she's so disfigured it's hard to tell,' stated Harry panting from exhaustion after the digging.

'Yeah, I think you may be right,' replied Edward.

'Where now?' asked Harry.

Beth pointed about two metres away from the grave and urged Harry to start there. He plunged the heavy metal head of the shovel into the ground below not caring about the flowers on the surface. Harry soon got into a rhythm and before long, the shovel hit something with a thud. 'I think we have found something,' he said breathing really hard. Edward and Beth waited with anticipation. Beth tried to compose herself for the possibility that this could be her body. Harry got down onto his knees and started shovelling the soil away with his bare hands. He soon came across an old worn blanket and before he uncovered the body he paused. 'Beth, I think you need to look away for a second until we know what's underneath here,' he said firmly but gently.

Beth knew he was right as she answered, 'Yes, okay, I'll wait over here.'

Edward moved in closer and Harry pulled away the blanket. They both gasped in horror as they saw the corpse of a young teenage girl with her face and upper body decayed with insects devouring her flesh or what was left of it. Harry moved his head away instinctively and threw up all over the flower bed. Edward turned his head away as the scene was too putrid for his eyes to take in. Harry put one of his hands up over his mouth and nose as the stench was noxious, as he carefully trowelled away more earth to reveal the rest of the body. He saw the girl had long dark curly hair and she wore a blood stained T-shirt. Harry asked Edward if he recognised the girl and Edward softly said, 'Yes, I do.' Beth instantly knew what that meant and she couldn't help herself; she had to take a look.

Before Edward could stop her, she knelt down next to Harry and hesitantly peered over to the corpse below. She saw a young girl's blackened and blue half rotting face and noticed the curls of her matted hair. The smell did not affect her the same as Harry, but she withdrew her gaze quickly when she came across the eaten flesh and maggots. 'No, no, it can't be me,' she screamed. Harry covered both ears to mask Beth's hallowing sounds. Edward moved in next to her and pleaded for her to come away from the grave. Beth crawled away and wailed continuously. Harry moved a few metres further up the flower bed and began the process all over again. He knew they were running out of time.

No one noticed the black shapes that were now closing in on Beth and Edward. The frail moonlight shone on their pale agonised faces which were encasing their cold, lifeless eyes. Their bodies were withered and their clothes were torn. There were uneasy sounds falling from their thin lips with utterances and moans. There was one amongst them who lingered slightly in the background, and he appeared to be taller than the rest. He seemed to be sniggering, and his hands were clasped together as if he was anticipating something.

32

Brian raced around the house gathering clothes and some personal items including important documents. He pulled a suitcase down from the wardrobe and piled in his belongings. His plan was to head south and cross over the English Channel where he would catch a train to Spain and hide out for a while. He would get to the bank before embarking on the ferry, and he had enough money to last him until he could figure out what to do next. Before leaving Brian decided to check his shed once more to see if there were any items he wanted to take with him. He placed his suitcase at the front door and went out for one last walk across Cedar Lane to his well-loved allotment. As he walked over the road, he could see something at the top end of the allotment. As Brian got closer, he could see that there was a person digging up his precious flower beds. He sneaked into the allotment and went behind his shed. Harry was too busy digging, and Edward was more concerned about Beth to even notice the presence of Brian coming up behind Harry. Before Harry could defend himself, Brian swung a large wooden paling against the back of Harry's head. Harry felt the pain radiate throughout his brain as he collapsed on the pile of cold earth. Edward left Beth and quickly knelt beside Harry's limp frame. 'Jesus, Harry, are you okay? Talk to me please, Harry,' cried Edward hysterically. Harry moaned and Edward saw the dark black liquid run from Harry's skull. 'Harry, please get up, he's going to kill you if you don't,' screamed Edward. Harry tried to lift his head but felt his world spinning in a frenzy. He flopped his face back into the soft soil to rest.

Brian quickly looked around the allotment, but the place appeared free from any other intruders. *Who was this man? And what was he doing digging up my allotment?* thought Brian. *Maybe he is with the cops? In that case, I better make a run for it as there are sure to be others around.* He thought about laying in some more punches while the guy was obviously out cold, but he knew time was of the essence. Brian threw down the piece of wood and was just about to turn and run out of there when he felt a severe pain run up the back of his head. He placed one of his hands up to the crown of his head and felt a cold, gooey substance run furiously between his fingers and then he fell into a heap. Reverend Elizabeth breathed a sigh of relief as she put down the brick and ran straight over to Harry's lifeless body. She investigated the wound on Harry's head and pulled a large cotton scarf from around her neck and pressed it firmly on the gaping hole. The blood flow began to ease, and she felt for a pulse.

'Looks like I got here just in time, hey!' she said as she looked at Edward.

'You can see me?' replied Edward surprised.

'Of course, silly, they don't call me Reverend for nothing.' Edward then realised who she was and that Harry had said he had a good mentor who might be able to help them.

'I'm Edward. Pleased to meet you, Reverend,' replied Edward.

'I thought you might be, Harry has told me all about you and Beth,' replied Elizabeth.

'Will Harry be all right?' asked Edward.

'I think so, as the blood has stopped now. We will need to get him to the hospital though, to get him checked over,' replied Elizabeth. Both Edward and the Reverend then heard Beth's terrifying screams. Edward just remembered that he had forgotten all about her. He turned to where he had left her sobbing on the ground and saw Beth surrounded by the group of lost souls. 'Edward, help me please,' she cried. Beth was hunched up against the wooden shed, and the black shapes were encroaching closer and closer with every second. Their moans and groans were getting louder, and they thrashed from side to side. The large figure at the back was speaking in a strange language Edward had never heard before. The weird figure was raising his arms to the dark night sky as if he was summoning someone or something. Elizabeth's suspicions had been right; she knew that this was the demon she had discussed with Harry. Beth was in real danger; if she didn't act quickly, Beth would soon be at the mercy of this malevolent creature. The reverend swiftly stood up and started walking towards the shed. Edward tried to break through the mass of squirming black shapes to get to where Beth was, but it was impossible, there were too many of them. Beth closed her eyes and prayed for Edward to get there so he could help her escape.

The Reverend stopped a few meters away from the demon. By this time, he had known that she was walking towards him. He turned his head completely around without moving his body. The body belonged to a poor young boy, David Wilson, and his frail body was now made up of thin emaciated bones and David's face showed years of suffering and yearning to be free. The demon was not fussy, and this soul seemed a suitable vessel for the demon to be able to carry through his goal of reaching the afterlife. He wasn't about to let the Reverend get in his way. Elizabeth tried to remain calm; she had had some dealings with demons in the past but this particular predator, she thought was much stronger and cunning. She pulled out of her coat pocket a large crucifix and held it firmly in her right hand. 'Demon, I see thee,' she began. Her voice was loud and full of confidence. It was important that the demon sense no fear, as all demons feed off this human emotion and it's as if they grow stronger from it. The Reverend was not afraid; she had God on her side.

The foul body in front of her slowly twisted around and it spoke. 'Who art thee who dare call to me to show myself?' The demon sneered.

As the sounds left the dead man's mouth, they filled the night air with a strange black trail of vapour. The eyes of this once healthy young person were now black as coal and shining as if they had been dipped in a clear glossy varnish. The Reverend composed herself and replied. 'I am the Reverend Elizabeth, and I am here to banish you from that poor soul you harbour against his will. I command thee to go back to where you came from, you are not welcome here demon.' David's body began to distort and its legs grew and buckled backwards at his knees. Large grotesque claw-like pincers formed on each of his hands as the demon rose above the soil in the isolated allotment. Elizabeth gasped and tried to keep herself from running in the opposite direction.

Meanwhile, the groping souls were frozen giving Edward the chance to get near to Beth where he quickly ordered her to get back inside Brian's car. She closed her eyes and pictured herself being on the back seat of the car, and soon she found herself safely on the familiar back seat with Edward by her side. 'Edward, what is going on? And what's that thing out there?' she said.

Edward didn't want to frighten her more than she already was, so he just pretended that he didn't know. 'Will you be okay for a while if I go back out there and see if I can help the Reverend?' he asked.

Beth was scared and didn't want to be left alone but she knew the Reverend was in trouble and so she sighed as she replied, 'Okay, Ed, but please don't be long, I don't like being on my own, what if those things get in here?'

'They can't,' Edward replied confidently. 'I'll only be a little while and then I will be back here with you, I promise,' he said as he disappeared from the car. Beth found herself alone and frozen with fear as she curled up on the back seat of the car.

Edward made his way to Elizabeth's side and said, 'Look, Reverend, I may not have had any experience in dealing with demons, but I am here if you need me to help, if I can.'

The Reverend smiled and said, 'Thank you, Edward, you are very brave and for now, just being here with me is enough.' Elizabeth then pulled out a small leather bound bible from her other coat pocket and held it up with her left arm outstretched. 'Demon, you do not frighten me, I have the Lord here with me and he commands you to leave that poor soul's body, and go back to where you came.' Elizabeth then started to recite the Lord's Prayer, 'Our father who art in heaven, hallow be thy name, thy kingdom come thy will be done on Earth as it is done in heaven. Give us this day our daily bread and forgive those who trespass against us…'

With that, the demon roared and flew directly above the Reverend's head. Edward cowered as the beast used its great claws and hooked them both into Elizabeth's shoulders. Elizabeth's body began to rise from the ground, and the demon threw her several meters down the side of the allotment. Elizabeth's fragile body crashed hard onto the wooden fence. The demon let out a loud, piercing laugh and turned to the wailing figures that were by now clinging together around the wooden shed. He scanned the allotment for Beth and when he could not see her, the demon opened his vile lips and let out the most penetrating howl followed by a large swarm of flies that flew over the allotment like a black cloud. Edward knew he had to get back to Beth and try to get her somewhere safer. The demon was much too quick for Edward, and he arrived outside Brian's car before Edward could return. Edward tried to penetrate through the metal to get back inside where Beth needed him, but it was as if there was an invisible barrier around the vehicle. Edward could not break his way through. The demon opened his mouth and faced Edward. Suddenly Edward found himself being blown fiercely over to the allotment where he was pinned to the roof of the wooden shed. His arms and legs were heavy, and he could not move his head. He was paralyzed. 'Oh, Jesus, Beth, get out of there and run,' he shouted with all his might.

Beth lay still curled up in the foetus position on the back seat of Brian's car. She didn't dare open her eyes, in case, she caught sight of the black things and worse—if she saw that creature. Beth heard a tapping on the glass as she lay there shaking in dread. 'Oh no, I'm not going to look, it's going to be those fucking creeps.'

The demon spoke, 'Come now, child, do you not want to speak with me? I have important things to tell you, and I can make sure you get what your heart desires.'

Beth squeezed her eyes shut even tighter as she heard the words of the demon. She felt a weird sensation overcome her whole being as he continued to speak through the window of the car. 'I do not want to hurt thee, child, I have a quest, and you can be of great help to me. I will in return grant you the one thing that you do not have and that is life.' Beth sensed the feelings growing stronger in her gut, and she felt her eyes open without her consent. Her body forced her to sit upright and face the demon who was for now kneeling on the pavement outside. Beth looked into the mesmerising black eyes of the creature, and she didn't feel afraid anymore, in fact, she felt drawn to this monster, against all of her intuition. The demon continued, 'I have the power to get you what you want, child. I know thee was taken away from this world too soon. I know thee wishes to be amongst the living once more.' Beth could not resist his voice, it was truly enchanting. 'Just come with me now and I can make that happen,

I promise that no harm will come to thee. You will need to do something for me first and in return I will give thee back your life.' The demon sniggered and couldn't help licking the frost off the glass with his huge purple tongue. Dark phlegm was dripping from the corners of his thin scaly lips. The demon knew it was nearly time for Beth to return to the light and that if she allowed him to enter her soul, he too would be carried back to the afterlife. This was his main purpose and, of course, his words to Beth were not to be trusted. He had no interest in Beth's needs. She was just another vessel to him, and once used, he would discard her like all the rest. All the demon needed was for Beth to leave the safety of her car, and once she was on the pavement, Beth would be easily possessed.

Edward writhed to and fro trying to release his body from the invisible restraints. It was no use; he just couldn't break free. He shouted to Beth, Harry and the Reverend, in case, they could hear him. Harry began stirring and staggered to his feet. He looked around and carefully listened for the voices of Beth and Edward. Vaguely he heard Edward's voice although it was low in tone and seemed very weak. Harry began shouting for Edward. Edward heard Harry's call and shouted as loud as he could, 'I'm on the roof of the shed, Harry, help me.'

'What are you doing up there, Edward? Is Beth with you?' replied Harry.

'Harry, the demon put me here, and Beth is in the car but he is trying to coax her out of it.'

Harry noticed the group of dark figures crouched around the shed and they seemed dormant somehow. He started to walk towards the gate of the allotment. As he crossed the road, he saw a large dark figure knelt down at the side of Brian's car. Harry shouted over to the fiend, 'Hey, leave that girl alone, you piece of shit.' The demon pulled his head away from the window and cracked his neck several times before he rose to his feet. Harry was now underneath the lamppost and standing directly in front of the evil presence. He felt fear throughout every pore of his skin, and he remembered what Elizabeth had told him. Harry thought about Beth and this somehow distracted him from the fear he was feeling. Harry looked right into the demon's soulless eyes and spoke, 'We drive you from us, whoever you may be, unclean spirits, satanic powers, infernal invaders, wicked

135

legions, assemblies and sects. In the name and by the virtue of Our Lord Jesus Christ. May you be snatched away and driven from the Church of God and from the souls redeemed by the Precious Blood of the Divine Lamb.' The demon lurched forward and effortlessly launched Harry's body into the air, and with an expansive screech, the demon tossed Harry's defenceless body down on top of the car. Harry landed face down with his legs and stomach hitting the cold metal surface of the car's roof whilst his face, chest and arms crashed into the front windscreen shattering the glass into a thousand pieces. Harry's cut and bleeding face was all Beth saw before she screamed. Harry lay there motionless with gashes and cuts strewn all over his face and blood slithering down his skin. The demon snarled and continued to lure Beth from her place of safety.

33

Edward felt useless, pinned to the wooden roof and could only shout at the Reverend in hopes that she would hear him. 'Reverend Elizabeth, you've got to get up and go and help Harry. He's hurt really bad, and the demon is going to get Beth. Please, Reverend, wake up!'

Elizabeth moved her sore head and scanned the rest of her body. She could feel some aches and shooting pains in her legs, but her arms felt okay to move. Elizabeth heaved herself up with the aid of the fencing and stood on her shaky legs. She gazed around the allotment and saw the lifeless body of the man who had attacked Harry. She saw the group of withering souls nestled together over by the shed and Edward pinned on the rooftop. She called to him and slowly put one bruised foot in front of the other. 'I'm okay, Edward; I'm here now, are you okay?'

Edward shouted down, 'I'm fine but please help Beth and Harry.'

'Okay, I'm on my way,' replied Elizabeth.

As she left the allotment, she could see the demon positioned on the roadside. Beth's face was leering from inside the car. She could not see Harry until she crossed the road and stepped into the pale orange glow of the street lighting. As she crept closer, Elizabeth gasped as she saw Harry's unconscious body. She heard Beth's cries as the interior of the car filled with a deathly vapour from the demon's mouth. The mist soon turned to thousands of tiny black flying insects that covered Beth and the back seat. Beth swiped her hands in front of her face uncontrollably to clear her eyes and mouth.

'Please stop,' she cried.

'Demon,' shouted Elizabeth. 'You don't belong here.' Elizabeth quickly tied herself to the metal lamppost with the belt of her coat and took hold of her small bible. She began hastily to recite the prayer which she hoped would banish this demon forever, but she knew this particular thing was stronger than any other she had encountered.

Poor Harry, Elizabeth thought, *this is my fault, he was not ready and I made him confront this beast, oh, Harry, I'm sorry.* Elizabeth knew she did not have much time before this brute would stop her, but she began to utter the rest of the prayer that Harry had started earlier, 'Cease by your audacity, cunning serpent, to deceive the human race, to persecute the Church, to torment God's elect, and to sift them as wheat. This is the command made to you by the Most High God, with whom in your haughty insolence you still pretend to be equal.'

The demon immediately turned its horrific head and smiled. 'You can't banish me, who art thee but a useless wench.' He opened his great cumbersome dangling arms and raised them to the sky. Large dark clouds began to form and swirl, and the winds began to strengthen. Great bursts of lightning flashed down upon Elizabeth, and she shrank in fear. The demon laughed and directed the winds towards her, and Elizabeth felt the metal post move underneath her. The post began to sway backwards and forwards and with one gigantic gust of wind, it crashed heavily into the roof of Brian's house and pulled a section of bricks with it. The demon laughed in triumph and made its way back to Beth who was by now a hopeless wreck.

Elizabeth didn't give up; she undid the belt and crawled a few paces nearer to the car and retied her belt to the metal railings which were unscathed. She continued her prayer shouting out every word, 'The God who will have all men to be saved, and to come to the knowledge of the truth. God the Father commands you. God the Son commands you. God the Holy Ghost commands you. Christ, the Eternal Word of God made Flesh, commands you.'

'You don't give up easily, bitch,' said the demon as he turned once more to face her. Elizabeth felt the railings lift from the ground and she went hurling with them across the gardens and crashed into one of the neighbour's front windows. Glass exploded everywhere, and Elizabeth's body was tangled between railings. She lay there unconscious.

Harry began to wake and felt an enormous pain in both his legs and quickly put his hand to his stinging face. The trickles of blood had dried and Harry managed to stick hold of the interior of the window frame and slide his legs down to the ground. He felt nauseous and dizzy but was able to stand. He shouted to Beth, 'Where are you?' but he heard no reply. He saw no sign of the beast and tears began to well up in his eyes. He looked over across the desolate road and saw the demon figure walking along the flower beds. Harry hobbled across the cold tarmac surface and crept silently through the allotment gates.

Edward shouted to him, 'Harry, he's got Beth, stop him please!'

'Where are you, Edward?' answered Harry in a distraught voice.

'I'm pinned to the roof of the shed, I can't get free. You're her only hope now, Harry, please hurry.'

Harry trampled on the flower beds and reached the demon who was now standing at the foot of Beth's grave. He was mumbling to her and Harry could not make out the words. Harry called out once more to Beth hoping she would hear him, but Beth was in a trance-like state, and no one could help her now. *It's too late, she's gone, that bastard has possessed her,* Harry thought. His legs gave way, and he knelt down in the damp dirt beneath him.

'Don't give up, Harry,' shouted Edward, but Harry knew he was beat. His body was weak and he couldn't move his legs, he was stuck in the soil. Edward looked up to the sky and prayed, 'Please, God, don't let Beth be taken away, she's a good kid and doesn't deserve this,' he cried.

Suddenly a golden globe of light descended over Beth and the demon froze as Michael stood beside her. 'Yes, demon, I know thy name, and you do not belong here,' said Michael calmly. The demon backed away and screeched and moaned. 'Zakan is thy name, and you are not welcome here in this realm.' Zakan, from the old worlds, who enslaved the poor and meek. 'You were cast out and banished by your kin and sought a life of misery and evil. I know thee well,' continued Michael. The demon was powerless.

Michael opened his arms and a large ball of white light emerged which moved towards the demon shape. Harry lifted his head at this point and saw the light penetrate the dark eerie figure. In an instant, the demon was gone and the remnants of

David Wilson's body, that had been its host, collapsed on the ground.

Harry shouted out to Beth, who was by now aware once more. 'I'm over here with Michael,' she shouted.

Edward felt the huge weight lifted from his limbs and he was soon stood next to Beth. 'Thank you, Michael, for saving her,' Edward said. 'Thought you'd had it there, kid,' said Edward teasingly.

Beth just smiled and they both giggled. Harry stood up on his feet and looked around for his friend. 'The Reverend was strong but the demon was too big of a match for her,' said Edward. 'I think she is over by the houses.'

Harry limped across the road and saw the destruction before his eyes. He saw the half-demolished house and further down the street he could see the windows smashed inwards. He called out to Elizabeth. She replied, 'I'm over here, Harry.' Harry found her enmeshed between the window pane and metal palings. Her legs were twisted, and she had cuts on her arms and face but she was breathing. 'Harry, I'm so sorry, I am glad you are okay,' Elizabeth said.

'It's okay, Rev, just rest and I'll get you some help.' Harry noticed the lights were on throughout the whole of Cedar Lane. He knocked on a door and asked if he could use their phone.

Harry quickly dialled 999 and asked for two ambulances as he remembered that Brian was still out cold in the garden beds. He then phoned George. It was early in the morning, however, George did not sleep much anymore. He heard the ring almost instantly and picked up the receiver, 'Hello, George speaking,' he said in a rough voice.

'George, it's Harry, you better get out to Cedar Lane as I think we've got the bastard,' said Harry. 'He has buried the girls in his own backyard, George, can you fucking believe it?'

'What! Are you winding me up, Harry?' replied George as he perched on the edge of his bed.

'No, really, George, it's a long story but you better get your team down here as soon as possible to corner off the street and check out the remains.'

'Okay, Harry, I'm on my way.' Harry put the telephone down and thanked the concerned neighbour. Harry told her that the police were on the way and to stay indoors, but everything was okay, and she was safe. Harry returned to Elizabeth's side and waited for the ambulance. Her breathing was shallow but she held onto his hand tightly. Once Elizabeth had been carefully transferred into the back of the ambulance, Harry went back to the allotment. By this time, George had arrived and was checking out the burial ground. It looked as if Brian was still alive as Harry saw his body being taken into the second ambulance which left almost immediately.

'Jesus Christ, Harry! I don't fucking believe it. The bastard buried the girls right under our noses,' said George sucking hard on his cigarette. 'How did all this happen, Harry?' he inquired.

Harry knew Beth would be leaving soon, and he didn't want to miss the opportunity of saying goodbye. 'George, I got to be someplace, but I promise I'll tell you everything tomorrow or later on today.'

George seemed too occupied with the scene and making sure his constables were doing what they should be doing. 'Okay, Harry, be in my office today no later than eleven, you hear me?'

'Sure do,' replied Harry grinning from ear to ear.

'See you then,' replied George as he threw his cigarette butt down and walked away.

Harry found Michael waiting near the damaged car. He heard both Beth and Edward's voices as he approached. 'Harry, it's nearly time for me to go, but I have one last favour to ask of you,' said Beth.

'Okay spill,' replied Harry.

'Michael has given me permission to go see my parents and Tina for one last time, and I was really hoping you would be there to talk to them for me?'

Harry stood back in shock as he knew this would not be easy for Beth. 'Of course, I will be there with you,' he replied.

'Good, well, let's get going,' Beth said as she turned to look for Michael's approval. Michael nodded, and both Edward and Beth visualised themselves in the back seat of Harry's Mini.

34

Harry pulled into the long and somewhat familiar driveway of 185 Birch Lane. It was early in the morning with the sun beginning to peep over the hilltops, but he figured time was not important at moments like these. Edward turned to Beth and gave her a reassuring smile. 'You going to be okay with this, Beth?' he asked kindly.

'No, I don't think I will be, but I couldn't go without saying goodbye,' replied Beth.

'It will be great for me to see my big sister Jane too,' he said with a grin, trying to make light of the situation.

Beth just smiled back at him, as they both closed their eyes and found themselves in Beth's front room. Tina was jumping up and down like crazy as she saw Beth first. 'Oh, my baby girl, you can see me can't you?' said Beth. Tina just twirled and twirled in excitement. Meanwhile, Harry knocked softly on the front door. James heard the noise first, as he really did not sleep much since Beth had gone missing. Jane had sleeping tablets which helped her get a few hours of rest. He slowly walked down the stairs of the unit and opened the door. Harry apologised for waking him so early in the morning but explained that it was very urgent, and he needed to talk to both Jane and James. Beth's father invited Harry in and ushered him to the front room while he woke his wife. 'Harry, Tina can see me and she's really excited about it!' laughed Beth.

'That's wonderful, Beth, I'm glad that makes you feel happy.'

Harry sat nervously on the edge of the sofa and waited for Beth's parents. He had no idea if they would believe him or not, but he was here for Beth and that was all that mattered. *I just hope he doesn't hit me, that's all,* he thought. Jane quietly entered the room with James holding his arms around her. She looked tired and frail. Beth saw how upsetting this must be for them both. She felt a deep sadness in the pit of her stomach which moved towards her heart. Harry waited until they were both seated and then cleared his voice. 'Thank you for seeing me at such a strange hour of the day,' he began.

'Do you have some news about my daughter?' asked Jane.

'I do, Mrs Cotten,' replied Harry. 'I am so very sorry to have to be the one to tell you both, but they found your daughter's body this morning.'

Jane let out the loudest wail, and James hugged her instantly. 'No. No, not my baby!' howled Jane.

Harry paused and reached over to place his hand on Jane's. 'I am so very sorry, Mrs Cotten, I wish I was here with better news.'

Jane began weeping, and Beth started to cry too. 'Oh, Mum, I'm so sorry, I did not want to see you hurt like this,' Beth cried. Edward tried to console Beth, but it was futile; she sobbed and sobbed.

Harry knew it was not the right time to continue, so he suggested making some tea. He made his way down the hallway towards the small, very equipped kitchen at the back of the unit. He found the kettle and managed to make three cups of hot tea. He found a small round tray and placed the beverages on it and carried it carefully back to the front room. James was stroking the back of Jane's head, and she was wiping her tears from her face. 'I'm sorry, Harry, I knew she was gone but hearing those words just confirmed my worst nightmare,' said Jane.

'No need to apologise, Mrs Cotten,' replied Harry, as he passed her the cup of hot tea. She sipped a few mouthfuls and then placed the cup on the side table.

'What happened to her?' asked Mr Cotten.

Harry spoke again softly, 'She was murdered,' replied Harry.

Jane lashed out, 'I hope you catch the bastard,' she said.

'Do you remember me from when I came with the police?' Harry asked. They both nodded. 'I don't know if you believe in this sort of thing, but I am a psychic, and your daughter found me. I can't see her, but I can hear Beth very clearly. She led me to the killer's house, and we found out where he had buried Beth and four other young girls as well.' Beth's parents looked at Harry with their mouths gaped open. 'I know this is rather a lot to take in, but it's true,' said Harry wishing there was hole he could disappear into. 'Your daughter has a relative with her called Edward and he says he is your baby brother, Jane.'

Jane gasped out loud, 'Oh, Eddie, my God, my sweet little Ed.'

Harry spoke again. 'Edward and Beth discovered the killer, and the police now have him in custody. Well, he is in hospital at the moment, but he will soon be in jail, where he will rot.'

'Did my baby suffer, Harry?' asked Jane.

'Mrs Cotten, please don't be alarmed, but your daughter and Edward are both here with me, and they would like to talk to you,' said Harry, ready for Beth's father to grab him by the scuff of his neck and sling him out of the unit. Surprisingly Beth's dad said nothing and Jane nodded.

Beth told Harry what to say. 'My beautiful mum and dad, I am okay, and I want you both to promise me that you will not be sad for me. I am always near you, and I love you both with all my heart and soul. I always have and always will do.' Beth tried to stop the tears from streaming down her face, and she tried to carry on talking despite the large lump building in her throat. 'I want you both to know that I am not in any pain and that I am being looked after by Edward. I want to thank you both so very much for being the best mum and dad I could have ever wished for. Please don't be sad, I want you to enjoy your lives and one day we will be together again, I promise.'

Jane burst into tears and Harry saw Beth's father crumble into the sofa no longer able to console himself. 'Thank you, sweetheart,' said Jane. 'You brought so much love and joy into our world, and we want you to know that we love you with all our heart and soul and always will do.'

Harry continued to repeat Beth's words out loud. 'Mum, Dad, I have to go know, but I will always be around you and sending you all my love.'

Beth's parents both said goodbye to their little girl, and Harry made his apologies once more and let himself out.

35

It was silent outside on the driveway. Harry knew Beth would be a while longer making the most of her last visit. 'Thanks, Harry, for doing that, I know it can't have been easy for you,' said Edward who had now joined Harry.

'It was the hardest thing I've ever had to do, Ed, and I don't ever want to do it again,' replied Harry.

Soon Beth appeared, and she also thanked Harry from the bottom of her heart. 'Harry, you don't know what it means to me to be able to say goodbye today,' she said.

Harry couldn't speak as he was fighting back the tears. Michael arrived, and Beth knew it really was time to go. 'Are you willing to come with me this time, Beth?' he asked. Beth nodded. 'Thank you, Harry, for all your help. We couldn't have done this without you,' said Edward who was also fighting back his own emotions.

'Yes, Harry, you are the best, thanks again, I mean it,' said Beth. 'I'm a little nervous, Ed,' she said.

'Don't be, you will be okay with me,' replied Edward as he smiled affectionately.

'Do I get to see these two Lara-kins before they go?' asked Harry.

Michael smiled and said, 'I don't see why not; that's not against any rules in my book.' They all laughed out loud. Suddenly Beth's image began to appear, and Harry could see a beautiful young girl with thick chocolate brown curls that bounced right past her shoulders. She had the bluest eyes and a fair complexion. Beth beamed one of her smiles, and Harry truly sighed in awe as that smile was the most beautiful thing he had ever witnessed. Harry looked down at her Pink Floyd T-shirt and her blue jeans. 'Wow, you are gorgeous, Beth, and your photograph at the station doesn't do you any justice. I'm so glad I met you,' Harry said lovingly.

'Well, thank you, Harry, you're not too bad yourself,' she giggled.

Harry turned to see a young teenage boy beside Beth who had tight-fitted black trousers and pointed shoes. His hair was golden blonde, and he had the same mesmerising eyes as Beth. 'Well, take a look at you,' Harry said. 'You are one cool dude, Ed.'

'Catch you later, Harry, and be good!' replied Edward with his usual cheeky grin spread all over his young face. Harry knew this would be his last chance to say goodbye. 'Thank you guys, I really loved meeting you both, and I will always remember you. Take care of each other and God Bless.'

'You too, Harry,' replied both Edward and Beth as they walked up the drive with Michael. Harry stood and watched them as they faded into the cool early morning light.